SPECIAL MESSAGE TO READERS

This book is published by

THE ULVERSCROFT FOUNDATION

a registered charity in the U.K., No. 264873

The Foundation was established in 1974 to provide funds to help towards research, diagnosis and treatment of eye diseases. Below are a few examples of contributions made by THE ULVERSCROFT FOUNDATION:

A new Children's Assessment Unit at Moorfield's Hospital, London.

•

Twin operating theatres at the Western Ophthalmic Hospital, London.

•

The Frederick Thorpe Ulverscroft Chair of Ophthalmology at the University of Leicester.

•

Eye Laser equipment to various eye hospitals.

If you would like to help further the work of the Foundation by making a donation or leaving a legacy, every contribution, no matter how small, is received with gratitude. Please write for details to:

THE ULVERSCROFT FOUNDATION,
The Green, Bradgate Road, Anstey,
Leicester LE7 7FU. England
Telephone: (0533)364325

SIX GUN WEDDING

The Dodd-Joel feud was over and, with one rancher's daughter marrying the other rancher's son, the hatchet would be well and truly buried. However, the Dodds and Joels and Lamont County's sheriff reckoned without the local rogues planning the theft of a wedding guest's priceless jewel, and the coming of a couple of professional killers hired to eliminate Gentle George, the guest from Kansas. In this double intrigue, the Texas Trouble-Shooters just had to get involved.

MARSHALL GROVER

SIX-GUN WEDDING

A Larry & Stretch Western

Complete and Unabridged

LINFORD
Leicester

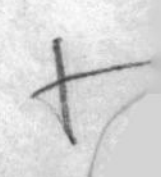

First published in Australia

First Linford Edition
published April 1994
by arrangement with
Horwitz Grahame Pty Limited
Melbourne, Australia

British Library CIP Data

Grover, Marshall
Larry & Stretch: six-gun wedding.
—Large print ed.—
Linford western library
I. Title II. Series
823 [F]

ISBN 0–7089–7502–X

Published by
F. A. Thorpe (Publishing) Ltd.
Anstey, Leicestershire

Set by Words & Graphics Ltd.
Anstey, Leicestershire
Printed and bound in Great Britain by
T. J. Press (Padstow) Ltd., Padstow, Cornwall

This book is printed on acid-free paper

1

The Death-Dealers

GEORGE MIDDLETON, junior cashier of the Reliance Bank of Shadlow, Kansas, entered the office of the county sheriff clumsily, almost measuring his length in fact. Sheriff Tim Phelan and Deputy Hershey shrugged resignedly. They were neither surprised nor exasperated when George tripped over the threshold, lurched in, overturned a chair, slumped against Phelan's desk and grasped its outer edge to steady himself.

Like most Shadlow citizens, the lawmen were familiar with George's problem. He wasn't drunk. Just naturally clumsy. A tanglefoot.

It was lunchtime in Shadlow. Phelan's lunch was on his desk. The deputy had finished eating a short time before.

Both lawmen were lean and in their 40's, Phelan being some five years Hershey's senior.

"Calling during my lunch break to tell you I'll be leaving town tomorrow," the cashier announced after regaining his balance. "I'm long overdue for a vacation and Mister Ellis has kindly agreed I should take advantage of this welcome invitation."

Phelan downed a well-chewed mouthful and surveyed George intently. In his mid-20's, the junior cashier was a personable young fellow, well-mannered, well-groomed in a colorless way, some 5 feet 9 inches tall, but looking shorter for a tendency to stoop. The face under the neatly-barbered sandy hair was average, not exactly homely, not exactly handsome.

"Let's take this a step at a time, young George," said Phelan. "You got leave due, so you're quitting town tomorrow — for how long?"

"Only for two weeks," said George. "This means I'll have ample time to travel to Nebraska for the wedding and . . . ”

“If you aren’t back in Shadlow by the twenty-fifth, a lot of Shadlow citizens are gonna be disappointed, and that includes me,” declared Phelan. “You’re the only prosecution witness in the county’s case against Keesing, and don’t you forget it. Nobody else saw Keesing come out of that back room. Nobody else saw Ed McQueen in the doorway, bleeding to death, pointing after Keesing and saying ‘Stop him.’ With Keesing claiming it wasn’t him you saw, it’ll come down to your word against his. Without you, we got no case.”

“But of course I’ll be returning to testify,” George hastened to assure him. “I haven’t resigned my position, Sheriff Phelan. I’m only taking leave due to me for the sake of attending a wedding which will become a happy family reunion.” He grimaced perplexedly. “What can that man Keesing hope to gain by his denials? I saw him so clearly."

"Killers have this habit of denying their guilt," growled Phelan. "Whereabouts in Nebraska, boy?"

"Lamont," grinned George. "The invitation arrived this morning — sent by my Cousin Myra, mother of the bride. She's considerably older than I of course. We've kept in touch over the years and . . . " His grin broadened, "this will be such a joyful occasion. A bond will be welded between the two most well-known ranching families of Lamont County, the Dodds and the Joels."

"Hold on now," interjected Stan Hershey. "I read a Nebraska paper a few months ago and there was this report of a feud in Lamont county and, by Judas, those were the names. The Dodds and the Joels."

"There was a feud," nodded George. "But that's all in the past. My cousin by marriage, Yancey Dodd, and Mister Ralph Joel, father of the bridegroom, have buried the hatchet. All is peace in that territory now. Well, what else could they do but shake hands and forget their differences? I mean, with Max Joel and second cousin Mary Sue becoming betrothed." He eagerly displayed a stage line ticket. "See? I've already been to the depot and booked my passage."

"All right, I got no authority to stop you leaving, but you heed what I'm telling you now, young George," frowned Phelan. "You got an obligation, know what I mean?"

"I'm fully conscious of my duty as a concerned citizen of this community," asserted George.

"Yeah, sure." The lawman gestured impatiently with a laden fork. "Look, boy, I know you mean to come back. You got good intentions, but you're a doggone tanglefoot."

"That's unkind, Sheriff," George said reproachfully. "I thought everybody knew I'm ashamed of my — uh — short coming — and very sensitive about it."

"You're just naturally awkward." Phelan wasn't about to spare his feelings. "You're the kind of young buck who'll walk right in front of a fast-moving wagon or trip and fall in front of a bunch of riders. Crazy accidents keep happening to you. Here in your hometown, folks are used to it. Everybody looks out for you. But when you start traveling north, it'll be different, won't it? Damn right — and likely dangerous."

"I'll be careful — extremely careful," George promised.

"I live in hopes," sighed Phelan. "Wire me as soon as you get there and look in on me soon as you get back."

"That'll be on the twenty-second for sure," said George, turning to leave.

To the sheriff's surprise, the young cashier managed to make his exit without bumping into anything.

"Mite jumpy, ain't you?" challenged Hershey.

"There'd have to be a wedding now

— of all times," fretted Phelan. "Hell, I don't want to spoil his fun. He lives so quiet, never causes trouble — except accidentally. Nice young feller, George Middleton. Like to see him good and settled with a wife to take care of him."

"She better not be the nervous type," grinned Hershey.

"He's entitled to go to a wedding and meet up with kinfolks, kiss the bride and have himself some fun," Phelan conceded. "I don't begrudge him his vacation. But — hell — I wish it was gonna be a Shadlow County wedding."

"You worry too much," shrugged the deputy, as Phelan resumed his lunch.

This observation triggered a grim response growled between mouthfuls; the sheriff was eating too quickly and to the detriment of his digestion. The murdered rancher, Ed McQueen, had been a good friend of his. Though it was not his prerogative to rule on Bob Keesing's guilt or innocence, he was in no doubt his old friend had been fatally stabbed by his own foreman.

"Keesing made a bad mistake," he insisted between sips of coffee for which he had no taste. "Five stab wounds, so he was sure Ed was dead. But Ed had strength enough to get on his feet and stumble to the doorway and point at his killer. And, if that night hadn't been so hot . . ."

"It was a couple of hours after midnight that Middleton came by the back of Schroder's place," Hershey reminded him.

"Right," nodded Phelan. "Young feller couldn't sleep, so he's out walking — at that hour."

"What was McQueen doin' in town that time?" frowned the deputy. "I keep forgettin'."

"Rode in to see the dentist," said Phelan. "Had a tooth pulled, felt too blame miserable for riding back to his spread, so Mike Schroder let him use the back bedroom above his saloon. Wasn't for that damn tooth, Ed might still be alive." He drained his cup and said bitterly, "I can't guess Keesing's motive, but there's no doubt in my mind. He killed Ed and I mean to see him hang for it. His alibi isn't worth a lead dime and, with young George as his witness, Prosecutor Ames'll get him convicted. But . . . " He grimaced irritably, "George is our ace in the hole. Without his evidence, there'll be no case. And the thought of Keesing going free makes me sick to my stomach."

"Not much of an alibi," Hershey agreed.

"At Bible they told me he rode out at midnight to check the north quarter," Phelan said scathingly. "You ever hear of a foreman going so far by himself, claiming he'd heard talk of rustlers? If there'd been any rustling hereabouts, he'd have sent hired hands out and he wouldn't have waited till midnight — and he wouldn't go it alone. But that's how I found him. Alone. No witnesses to swear he'd never left home range. He calls that an alibi? It's no alibi at all."

The waitress from a nearby diner arrived at this point, toting a cloth-covered tray. She would have been delighted to deliver the prisoner's lunch personally; Bob Keesing, an arrogantly handsome six-footer, had stirred the emotions of many a woman of this territory. Phelan disappointed her, and not for the first time, brusquely ordering her to surrender the tray to Hershey. The girl retreated in chagrin and, unhurriedly, Hershey carried the tray up the spiral staircase to the first floor cellblock, only one cell of which was occupied at this time.

While the prisoner satisfied his appetite, Hershey satisfied his curiosity regarding the visit of the star witness: Keesing had been watching from his cell window when George Middleton crossed Main Street.

"Thought you'd want to know," remarked the deputy.

"More important that *she* knows," was Keesing's muttered rejoinder.

"I guess you want me to . . . began Hershey.

"She pays you good for playing go-between," shrugged Keesing. "You know what to do — and it ought to be done today."

"I'll be headed her way in a little while," Hershey assured him. "Phelan's sendin' me out to Rockin' Seven. Seems he's leery of Guthrie's new hired hand, so I got to check him against a dodger in our files."

"That'd be a laugh on old psalm-singin' Guthrie," grinned Keesing. "A wanted man on his payroll. If it's true, he'll likely bust out crying."

"Got to travel Bible's high ground to get to the Guthrie spread," said Hershey.

"She'll be there," Keesing said confidently.

"There's a way I can signal her," said Hershey. "I can't risk bein' seen with her, but we got this signal."

"Yeah, fine," nodded Keesing. "So go earn yourself some easy money."

En route to Rocking Seven some two hours later, the deputy lit a small fire on the saddle of a ridge in sight of the distant Bible ranch-house. He found damp leaves and brush to toss on that fire to ensure a show of smoke. This was the signal that prompted the new widow, the new owner of Bible, to don riding clothes and order a hired hand to ready her horse.

A short time later, the blond and beautiful Belle McQueen rendezvoused with the go-between and listened to his report. Money changed hands after which she returned to the ranch headquarters to prepare for a journey. Hershey rode on to the Rocking Seven, interrogated Guthrie's new man, compared his appearance and general description with a *Wanted* bulletin and assured the rancher he had nothing to worry about. The resemblance noted by the sheriff was slight indeed; Guthrie's new man was a full three inches shorter and nowhere near as weighty as the on-the-run thief.

By midnight, Belle McQueen had arrived in Regansville, the next town northwest of Shadlow. She had located the men she needed to interview and had taken a room at the Bressart Hotel.

The poker party in the double room on the second floor had begun at sundown. It didn't break up until 1.45 a.m. The men sharing that room, Frenchy Cordeau and Carl Barris, farewelled the townmen who had boosted their joint bankroll and were having their last drink before retiring when the gentle knock at the door won their attention. They traded wary glances.

"Told you we're pushing our luck, staying on in this burg," scowled Barris. Like his partner, he favored the rig of the professional gambler, but there the resemblance ended. He was as blond as Cordeau was dark, two inches taller and, unlike Cordeau, running to fat. "That sore loser marshal — still leery of us."

"He's got nothing on us," retorted Cordeau, rising, tucking his shirt into his pants. "He had to turn us loose."

"Lack of evidence, sure," nodded Barris. "But we oughtn't have hung around."

"There were other pickings here," Cordeau reminded him. "This was a successful poker party for us. An extra seven hundred — the easy way." He frowned at the door as the knock was repeated. "Go ahead. See who that is."

Barris moved to the door, opened it and frowned uncertainly. Their nocturnal visitor was expensively gowned. The hat was fashionable and her veil completely concealed her features. The voice was soft, but compelling.

"May I join you, gentlemen?"

"Party's over, lady," said Barris.

"I'm aware of that," she nodded. "I waited — very patiently — for the other men to leave. Well? May I come in?"

"Ask the lady in, Carl," Cordeau smoothly urged.

"Well, okay," shrugged Barris, gesturing for her to enter. "But that was a long party. A man needs his sleep."

"It's a business matter," the woman told Cordeau, as she seated herself.

"We're a couple of sporting men," offered Barris. "Poker's our business, Miss . . . ?"

"You have other talents of which I'm well aware," she said briskly. "No need to introduce yourselves, gentlemen. I know who you are."

"And you?" prodded Cordeau.

"I prefer to remain anonymous," she murmured.

"That's kind of one-sided, lady," muttered Barris. He perched on the edge of the bed nearest her chair and lit a cigar. "Something you'd better understand. We have to know who's hiring us."

"Is that absolutely necessary?" She put the question to Cordeau while delving into her reticule. "Perhaps, for what I'm prepared to pay . . . "

"How'd she get onto us?" Barris demanded.

"We're acquiring a reputation, Carl," Cordeau reminded him. "The Reganville paper gave us quite a spread — and the lady obviously read that special edition."

"I had heard of you on other occasions," she declared, proffering a wad of banknotes.

Cordeau took the money, tallied it and whistled softly.

"A thousand," he told Barris.

"That's an advance," said the woman. "Another thousand will be mailed to any address you nominate — after you've earned it."

"Two thousand you're willing to pay?" challenged Barris. "Just how many citizens do we have to take care of for that kind of money — and how do we know you'll mail the other half?"

"You have my word," she shrugged, as Cordeau pocketed the wad. "If I'm trusting you with so generous an advance, surely you can trust me to forward the balance of the fee, a fee I've nominated. In reply to your first question, Mister Barris . . . " She held up a finger, "just one."

"I think the lady's proposition is reasonable, Carl," drawled Cordeau.

"All right," said Barris, nodding to her. "You got a deal."

"It will be necessary for you to leave Reganville tomorrow morning," she said. "Any objections?"

"None, smiled Cordeau. "And now all we need is a name, a description and, of course, we have to know the whereabouts of the party concerned."

"The name is George Middleton." She offered a description of the junior cashier of the Reliance Bank, also other information obtained from Deputy Hershey. "He'll be on the northbound stage from Shadlow leaving tomorrow morning. His destination is Lamont, Nebraska, a quite well-known town I believe."

"Yes, madam," nodded Cordeau.

"Anything else we ought to know?"

"Such as just where you want it done?" prodded Barris.

"I leave that to you," she said. "En route, perhaps, or at Lamont. It's only important that he never makes the return journey."

"You won't change your mind, identify yourself?" frowned Barris.

She shook her head and rose to leave. Cordeau coughed apologetically.

"Aren't we forgetting something?" he asked.

"About the other thousand," said Barris. "How do we get in touch?"

"That can be settled here and now if you're agreeable," she offered. "When you've completed your end of our little bargain, would it be convenient to return to Reganville and stay at this same hotel?"

"We could do that," said Cordeau.

"By the end of the month you'll receive a package containing ten hundred dollar bills," she told him. "It will be addressed to you care of the hotel. Will that be satisfactory?"

"Quite satisfactory, thank you," said Cordeau conducting her to the door.

He ushered her out in courtly fashion, then pulled the door almost shut. For a brief moment he stood there, watching carefully, pantomiming for Barris to stay quiet. Then he finished closing the door, hurried across the room and climbed through the window onto the second floor gallery.

For several minutes, Barris waited patiently. Cordeau was grinning complacently when he rejoined him.

"Don't tell me . . . I already guessed," said Barris. "She's right here in the hotel?"

"Last room along on this side," chuckled Cordeau. "Hell, she made it easy for me. Didn't lower the window shade until after she took the veil off."

"Didn't spot you?" prodded Barris.

"As far as she knows, she's still anonymous," said Cordeau. "But I got a good look at that face, Carl, a face we've seen before. Remember the Shadlow newspaper a couple weeks ago? Front page photographs of a rancher, his widow and his foreman?"

"I remember the names," said Barris. "Keesing, that's the foreman, has been charged with the murder of the rancher, McQueen."

"We've been retained to eliminate the only prosecution witness," Cordeau said elatedly. "And by who do you suppose?"

"That was the widow?" challenged Barris.

"Vanity, Carl," drawled Cordeau. "Never was a beautiful woman could resist a photographer. Mrs Belle McQueen probably enjoyed seeing her picture in the newspaper."

"What do you make of this?" asked Barris. Keesing's held for trial for knifing his boss — and the boss' widow pays us to wipe out the only witness against him?"

"Plain enough, I'd say," shrugged Cordeau. "The wife was cheating on the boss and Keesing's the other man. One of those triangle situations, Carl. And a break for us." He nodded vehemently. "Oh, sure. We'll earn the extra thousand, but that's not all. Chances are she'll inherit the McQueen ranch and get to be a wealthy lady."

"Now that we know who we're dealing with, we can put the arm on her for additional pay-offs," grinned Barris. "This thing has great possibilities."

"Exactly what I have in mind," nodded Cordeau. "Blackmail's an ugly word they say, but I've never thought so. Matter of fact . . . " He chuckled triumphantly, "it's one of my favorite words."

"We'd better turn in," Barris said briskly. "I'll be up early and checking timetables at the stage depot. By the time we've had breakfast, I'll know how far we have to travel to reach the next town on the north route."

* * *

In the hour before noon of the following day, two drifters of Texas birth were savoring the cooling waters of the North Loup River of Nebraska. A bend of river in an isolated area of Lamont County was just too seductive to be resisted by a couple of fiddlefoots weary of several days accumulation of trail-dust. On the south bank, their lunch of prairie chicken slowly cooked over a lazily smoking fire. Their unsaddled horses, a sorrel and a pinto, grazed contentedly and rested. Every item of their clothing, energetically laundered, hung drying on a clothesline improvised of a lariat. Their saddles were dumped, their cooking gear broken out. And now, naked as the day they were born, the veteran nomads wallowed in bliss. This was a Nebraska summer of extra high temperatures.

The taller Texan surfaced with his tow hair streaming about his face. Woodville 'Stretch' Emerson was aptly nicknamed, a cheerful beanpole of a man all of 6½ feet tall — minus boots.

"No steam risin' off our duds now," he observed. "Few more minutes and they'll be bone-dry. Then we eat, huh runt?"

"Then we eat," nodded his partner of better than 17 years, the brawny, dark-haired rugged Larry Valentine. "Chicken stew is fine for a change. Seems like we've been chewin' on jerky and jackrabbit for a week or more."

"Any idea where we're at?" enquired Stretch.

"Quien sabe?" shrugged Larry. "Somewhere in Nebraska — hot Nebraska. Some lonesome part of Nebraska. Else we couldn't take an all-over buck-naked bath."

"I guess we're a fair piece from any trail," remarked Stretch.

"We don't know that for a fact," said Larry. "Headed this-away from the northeast we didn't sight no trail, but that don't mean there ain't a trail."

"Which we'll go look for when we break camp," guessed Stretch.

"Best do that," agreed Larry. "I'm

near out of tobacco."

"And the only bottle we got is good for one stiff belt apiece," Stretch reminded him. "Reason enough for us to go look for a town, I reckon."

Privacy, peace and quiet and the aroma of their stewing chicken wafting toward them. What more could a couple of fiddlefoots wish for, especially two as trouble-prone as these? For longer than they cared to remember, the nomads from the Lone Star State had been wandering far and wide across the frontier, and with monotonous regularity, doing battle with every known variety of malefactor. Name any kind of rogue, the rustlers, the bandit gangs, the sharpers, cheaters, claim-jumpers, homicidal gunslingers; the Texas Trouble-Shooters had fought them all and were still surviving. Their oft-repeated claim to be peace-loving, bent on riding free and minding their own business, had become a bad joke. They didn't repeat it as often nowadays.

A short time later, having mutually agreed their clothing would be dry now, they began rising from the shallows. But then, with water lapping about their midriffs, they froze to gape at the rider slowly descending the shallow rise beyond their campside.

"Holy Hannah!" gasped Stretch.

The rider was female, young and pretty, a dark-haired girl straddling a smart-stepping bay colt, smiling, waving to them.

"Too late to get to our clothes," Larry said tensely. "She sees us already."

His voice shook. Irony of ironies, the survivor of a hundred and one life-or-death crises, strong on warrior instinct, cool-nerved in every perilous situation, was running short on courage at this moment, his morale nose-diving. Given a choice, either Texan would as soon have faced a Sioux war party or a band of kill-crazy outlaws than be descended upon by a member of the opposite sex in these embarrassing circumstances. They unfroze, loosed oaths and submerged to chin-level as, relentlessly, the young woman came on to rein up and dismount by their fire. Their embarrassment increased as, still smiling, she sauntered to the very edge of the bank to address them.

She didn't speak immediately. For what seemed a minute or more, she stood arms akimbo, laughing unrestrainedly, savoring their chagrin. Stretch winced uneasily. Not so Larry. He glowered at her; if looks could kill, she would have ceased breathing then and there.

She stood 5 feet 5 in her riding boots, a fine-figured brunette in light cotton blouse and divided riding skirt. Her headgear was practical, a real sun-shield, flat crowned, wide brimmed.

"Oh, how I hope to live to be a hundred," she declared when her mirth finally subsided. "It shouldn't be only children and grandchildren to whom I brag of this occasion. There should be great-grandchildren. Everything comes to she who waits.

Imagine little me stumbling on the famous Larry Valentine and his acutely embarrassed sidekick — under *these* circumstances!"

"Ah, hell, runt," groaned Stretch. "She knows us!"

"How long've you been spyin' on us, kid?" scowled Larry.

"Don't call me kid, call me Abby," she offered. "Short for Abigail. Full name Abigail Lilian Fenner, daughter of Milo Fenner, founder and editor of the Lamont *Pioneer*."

"She's a *scribbler's* daughter!" wailed Stretch. "That makes it *worse*!"

"How else would I so easily recognize you?" she taunted. "Of course, when I first saw you dismount and noted your generous height — well — that was a dead giveaway. Oh, yes. I was sure it had to be you."

"What in tarnation're you gonna do?" challenged Larry. "Stand there sassin' us all day?"

She chuckled again, moved closer to the fire and inspected the contents of the improvised cookpot.

"Smells good — and about ready for eating," she commented. "It'll be overcooked if you don't come out soon."

"We'd admire to come out and dry off right *now*," declared Stretch.

"And, naturally, I should turn my back," she smiled.

"I should hope," growled Larry.

"I won't do that," she blandly assured him. "I'll stand right here and watch you — to your intense humiliation — unless you agree to my terms."

"How d'you like the nerve of this gal?" Larry appealed to his partner. "Bad enough she comes snoopin'. Now she threatens us!"

"I've been very considerate of your feelings and your privacy until now, Mister Valentine," said Abby Fenner. "From the brush just along the bank, I watched you and, when it became obvious you intended washing your clothes and taking a bath, I moved back behind the rise. And I didn't peek."

"But now you're here," he accused.

"Now I'm here," she nodded. "And here I stay — looking at you — unless you swear to me, on your famous southern honour, that you'll grant my request. Your word is good enough for me, Mister Valentine. After all, your gallantry is as legendary as your courage and your remarkable luck."

"Here it comes," fretted Stretch. "You just know how it's gonna be, runt. Every time we give our word, we get ourselves in a whole mess of trouble."

"It's a simple request, a reasonable request," insisted Abby. "I don't see why it should cause you any trouble. Are you that nervous? Won't you at least listen?"

"You don't give us much choice," grouched Larry. "So okay, let's hear it."

"All I ask is that you come back to Lamont with me and meet Dad," she told them. "And I mean sociably. No abuse, no harsh words, no complaining about all you've suffered at the hands of the fourth estate. Yes, I know how you resent newspapermen, and maybe you're entitled. The *Pioneer* shows a tidy profit every so often by re-running a report of one of your adventures, but that's the business we're in."

"If it wasn't for scribblers like your pa, nobody'd know of us," Stretch said bitterly. "Doggone it, we never ever craved a reputation."

"You'll have to stifle your hostility and treat Dad with respect," she declared. "That's my offer, so what do you say? Is it yes? Or do I get to see my heroes in their natural state?"

"I ain't just humiliated, runt," mumbled Stretch. "I'm hungry!"

"You and me both," sighed Larry. "All right, Miss Smart-Aleck, you got our word. We'll come visit your old man."

"Thanks, Larry." She flashed him a smile and blew a kiss. "Won't take me a moment to tie my horse. Then I'll go sit with my back turned and I promise I won't look around until I have your permission."

"Now she's plumb polite," observed Stretch. "Now that she's got what she wants."

Abby Fenner led the bay to the grass, left it ground-reined beside Larry's sorrel and Stretch's pinto, found a flat rock and seated herself with her back to the bank. And she was as good as her word. Not till the Texans had emerged from the water, dried off and donned their clothes did she ask,

"Are you decent, yet?"

"Yup," grunted Larry.

"And feelin' a whole lot more comfortable," said Stretch.

When she rose and returned to the fire, the tall men were strapping on their sidearms and thonging their holsters down. Eager-eyed, she observed that other members of the fourth estate had been accurate on details. The taller Texan did pack a double load of the Colt product, his second .45 housed in the lefthand holster of a buscadero style shellbelt. And he still favored a pinto, while Larry preferred his sorrel and wore the one Colt slung to his right hip.

"Fetch your plates," she urged. "Let a lady dish up for you just this once. And if you happen to have a spare plate, oh my! this smells so *good*!"

They did have a spare plate. As Stretch brought their eating gear to light, Larry stared hard at Abby, the expression in his eyes intimidating her, though she masked her disquiet behind a cheery smile. Just what was he contemplating? She wondered about that and, fortunately for her composure, wasn't able to read his mind. For a long moment there, Larry was tempted to treat her as he had treated other impudent women who had tried his patience. Stretch half-expected he would do it again, would seize the girl, turn her over his knee and paddle her.

The temptation persisted for just that moment. Watching the fresh-faced, cheerful young woman ladling chicken stew onto tin plates, his ire cooled. She had embarrassed him, but he couldn't bring himself to retaliate. He wasn't about to fall in love with Abby Fenner, but he was certainly taking a liking to her.

And would he have cause to regret this?

2

Healthy Indignation

DURING that meal, the newspaperman's daughter assured the Texans their timing was perfect for a visit to the seat of Lamont County and maybe a stay of several days. Why so? Because of the feud. For a long time, up till a few months ago, the two biggest cattle spreads of this territory had been at loggerheads, Block D men trading shots with J Bar men as well as brawling with them in every saloon in town and often in the main street.

"But that's all in the past now, and doesn't that please you? I mean you've been so often quoted as victims of circumstance, always becoming involved in battles not of your choosing."

"And that's the truth," declared

Larry. "We never yet went lookin' for trouble — believe it or not."

"So rejoice!" she urged merrily. "This time, instead of becoming involved, you arrive when the truce has been declared."

"Rough while it lasted, huh?" prodded Stretch.

"Dad says it's a miracle there were no fatalities," she murmured. "There were wounded on both sides and, of course, more cracked ribs, loosened teeth and black eyes than our local doctors could keep count of. Also a stampede or two. Oh, yes, it was rough while it lasted. Even the presence of the one and only Sheriff Whitney was no deterrent."

"You talkin' about Big Bart Whitney?" frowned Larry. "*He's* sheriff of this territory?"

"Obviously you've heard of Lamont's resident celebrity," she remarked.

"Like we've heard of Bill Hickok, Bat Masterson and the Earps," nodded Stretch.

"And Cody and John Slaughter and all the other famous hombres," said Larry. "So Big Bart finally spooked these feudin' cattlemen into makin' peace?"

Abby set her empty plate aside, shook her head and reached for the coffeepot.

"It was love, not the Whitney influence, that settled the feud," she smiled.

"Love?" blinked Stretch.

"You must have *heard* of it," she teased, "no matter how woman-shy you are."

"Not woman-shy," Larry corrected. "Just marriage-shy."

They listened to her account of the end of the feud with keen interest. How *could* salty old Yancey Dodd, the Block D boss, continue warring with Ralph Joel of J Bar over rights to the waterhole between their two properties? How indeed, now that his only child, Mary Sue, was betrothed to the elder son of the same Ralph Joel? Both college-educated, handsome Max Joel and the comely Mary Sue had insisted on falling in love, feud or no feud, and the unpublicized courtship, in Abby's opinion, must have had the full support of their mothers; Myra Dodd and Amy Joel had chosen to ignore the feud and maintain their friendship.

"It was as much a clash of personalities as the disputed waterhole that started the feud," Abby opined. "Much as I love and admire Mister Dodd, he's a hard-boiled old hellion with what you'd call a hair-trigger temper, one of a kind you must have met often in your wanderings. A cattleman who came up the hard way, starting with almost nothing, fighting Indians and rustler gangs to hold his land and ending up as a successful and wealthy rancher? Sound familiar?"

"We've known many of his kind," nodded Larry.

"I think Mister Dodd's pugnacity was mostly to blame," she continued. "Right from the start he was suspicious of Mister Joel's correct speech and fine manners. Mister Joel, I should explain, is more the gentleman-rancher type. Come of good stock, as they say. His brother — I think his name is Lester — is a big success in Saint Louis and quite a social leader. Elroy told me his Uncle Lester owns the grandest restaurant in Saint Louis, the Cafe de Paris, patronized by only the high society folk."

"Who's Elroy?" asked Larry, as they started on their coffee.

"Elroy Joel, Max's brother," she said offhandedly. "He'll be best man to Max at the wedding — and no doubt winning the admiration of every love-starved spinster in attendance. Listen, we don't have to talk about Elroy. He's not important."

On rare occasions, the usually guileless Stretch could be as intuitive as his partner; this was one of those times.

"You get the feelin' this Elroy buck's been rufflin' Abby's feathers?"

"The idea just now crossed my

mind," drawled Larry.

Abby waxed disdainful.

"We're about the same age," she shrugged. "Elroy's quite a charmer, and always trying to court me. I think he's conceited. Now where was I? Oh, yes. I was going to mention Yancey Dodd also has a distinguished relative coming to Lamont for the wedding, his brother-in-law Jerome Chadwick, a quite famous and very rich lawyer of Denver, Colorado."

"Sounds like it'll be quite a shindig," remarked Larry.

"All very orderly, all very proper, if the Joels have their way," said Abby. "The reception will be held at the best hotel in town, the Savoy, owned by our mayor, Eugene Lingard."

While the Texans sipped coffee, they strove manfully to keep track of the many names voiced by informative Abby. The mayor of Lamont, they learned, had done much to steer his community along the path to progress and civilization — and the finer things of life. As well as owning the luxuriously-appointed Savoy Hotel, he had endowed a public library and an art gallery. Under his administration, Lamont had taken on the trappings of a frontier metropolis that would rival Omaha and Lincoln, and all this despite the feud that had raged so long.

Though Abby spoke of them at some length, though they memorized their names, they thought it unlikely they would rub shoulders with such notable locals as Yancey and Myra Dodd, parents of the bride, Ralph and Amy Joel, parents of the bridegroom, the redoubtable Sheriff Whitney or the management and staff of Mayor Lingard's Savoy Hotel. As Larry put it,

"You're talkin' about folks we'll likely never meet. We're only visitin' Lamont to keep our promise and howdy your old man. If we stay a night or two, we sure won't be stayin' at the mayor's fancy hotel."

"There's a hotel I'd specially recommend . . . " began Abby.

"Some bug-trap on the edge of town?" Larry challenged defensively. "Forget it. We ain't deadbeats."

"Might look broke, but we ain't," muttered Stretch.

This was true enough. The combined bankroll of the Texas drifters, snug in Larry's hip-wallet, tallied to a handy $400 at this time, thanks to recent successful gambling sprees in towns north and west of where they now found themselves. When down to their last few dollars, they turned their hands to all manner of chores; they were nothing if not versatile. But, when solvent, they drifted at will.

"You don't have to be so defensive," chided Abby. "The Hartigan Hotel on Lorring Street is no bug-trap, the rates are reasonable, the rooms comfortable and, what's more, it's conveniently located. I was just trying to be helpful."

"You're the clever lady that took advantage of us," Stretch reminded her. "So pardon us if we stay leery of you."

"Your old man'll write of us, tell the whole blame territory we've arrived," grouched Larry. "For us, that could mean trouble from your local layabouts, the kind of trouble we don't crave."

"You can discuss that with Dad," she offered. "He's a very reasonable man."

"But a scribbler," complained Stretch.

The coffeepot was empty. It was time to douse the fire, pack gear, saddle up and get moving again with Abby playing guide. As they started out, she remarked they would make the county seat inside the hour; the town trail was only a short distance away. Flanked by the tall riders, moving steadily along the trail, she got to talking again. They didn't mind listening. They had traveled in less appealing company and their initial resentment was wearing off.

"Quite a coincidence. My first chance to go riding in better than a week. I deliberately rode clear of the stage route, the railroad tracks and the cattle country because I wanted to be by myself for a while. And who should I stumble on? The heroes of my girlhood years!"

"Hark at her." Stretch grinned past her at his partner. "Girlhood years she says. Just as if she was of age."

"Twenty-one last birthday," she announced.

"I'd have figured maybe sixteen — seventeen," shrugged Larry.

"I could say the same of you two," she smiled. "I was still a schoolgirl, amusing myself getting under Dad's feet, poking around his office and exploring old editions, when I first saw a picture of you. Do you know you haven't change a bit? You don't look a day older."

"It's the booze," Larry said satirically.

"And the easy livin'," said Stretch.

"Dad insisted I'd been cooped up with him too long and needed fresh air," she murmured. "I guess he was right, but I'll be glad to get home, don't like to leave him to fend for himself. When they become widowers, men don't take proper care of themselves."

"How long since your mother died?" asked Larry.

"I was only ten," she said. "So I've had to look out for him ever since. I handle the cooking, help around the office. You'd be surprised how versatile a newspaperman's daughter can be. I've learned to set type, operate the press, even write up reports and sell advertising space."

"So you're Handy Abby, your old man's segundo," drawled Larry. "But don't it cut both ways?"

"Well, of course," she nodded. "Milo Fenner is the best father a girl could wish for — and don't you forget it, Larry Valentine. When you meet him . . ."

"Uh huh," he grunted. "Promised, didn't we? Don't worry. We'll show him respect."

"It's just we could respect him more," explained Stretch, "if he was a horse-breaker or a barber maybe or a good barkeep."

Their first sight of Lamont 80 minutes later made quite an impression on the much traveled Texans. They could not justly refer to this bustling metropolis as just another cattle town. Had there been street cars, paved sidewalks and electric lighting, they would have been reminded of Denver. Certainly Lamont, Nebraska, was taking on all the other trappings of progress. There were a great many brick buildings along Main Street and, for the most part, the townfolk were well-dressed, prosperous-looking. City Hall was an imposing edifice, as was the triple-storied Savoy Hotel. The stagecoach depot paled into insignificance when compared with the railroad depot about which porters and roustabouts were kept busy. Also impressive was the headquarters of the legendary Big Bart Whitney, a double-storied structure with shaded porch, bigger than average office and barred windows up top as well as at street level, indicating a second floor cellblock. No fewer than three church steeples were visible rising above the areas east and west of the heart of town. The Saloons? There looked to be dozens of them, and as many stores. Maybe the day of the general mercantile was passing; those observed by the newcomers were specialty stores, haberdashery, hardware, milady's fashions, gents' apparel, leathergoods and the like. Yes, the drifters were impressed, but sceptical too.

"I think this is what they call progress," was Larry's first comment.

"You suppose the barkeeps wear white jackets in this burg?" frowned Stretch.

"They got them telephone contraptions here?" Larry asked Abby.

"Telephones?" She flashed him a smile. "Not yet, but give us time. Lamont's coming on fast, I can tell you. Ever see a typewriter? We have one at the office. I use it all the time.

Genuine Remington, first model. And just wonderful."

"I wonder if the Remington outfit's still making guns," mused Stretch.

"Here we are," announced Abby.

They reined up at the hitchrail fronting the clapboard double storey building that was home to Milo Fenner and daughter and headquarters of the *Pioneer*. Abby dismounted lithely. The tall men followed suit, looped their reins and tagged her into the ground floor area dominated by the printing press, stacks of paper, shelves containing early issues, a couple of desks, a potbellied stove and innumerable chairs. The place had a lived in look. A door at the rear opened into a kitchen. Another door was half-open; the Texans glimpsed a bed and small table.

But these details were secondary to the small man in the wheelchair. He had their full attention and, at once, their sympathy was aroused. Wheeling himself away from the desk at which he'd been working, he looked them over, nodded cordially and remarked to his daughter,

"I fixed my own lunch. You were gone longer than you counted on, huh? Must be hungry now."

"I've had lunch," she assured him bending to kiss his balding pate. "Guess who invited me to share prairie chicken stew?"

"I don't have to guess," he grinned, eyeing the Texans again. "Know 'em anywhere. How'd you persuade 'em to pay me a visit? They don't socialize with journalists, the way I hear it."

"The feminine touch," bragged Abby. "It was bath day for these illustrious outlaw-fighters. I intruded on their noon-camp and threatened to ogle them in their naked state unless they promised to obey orders. As you can see, dear Dad, they promised."

"So then you kept your back turned," Milo Fenner assumed. "Well, for that I'm grateful, honey. I try to be liberal-minded, but I don't reckon I'd approve of my daughter gawking at a couple of buck-naked trouble-shooters." He accorded the frowning Texans another cordial nod. "Welcome to Lamont, boys. A little frustrating for you, this meeting, I imagine. I'm one editor you wouldn't want to assault or dunk in a water trough. As you can see, certain parties beat you to it."

"That's how this happened to you?" Larry asked quietly.

"That's how this happened to me," said the *Pioneer's* founder-editor.

Matching stares with this frail, crippled, but still good-humored newspaperman, the drifters showed their sympathy and concealed their bitter indignation. Milo's facial scars looked to have been recently inflicted. Maybe they would heal in time, or maybe he would carry them to his grave. His right arm was supported by a sling. His ribs were taped, his torso encased in a plaster corset; this they could see, his striped shirt being unfastened.

"Rough," commented Larry.

"The joke's on them," grinned Milo. "They took time to break my right arm, so I can't shake hands with you. Believe me, I'd like to. But it happens I'm lefthanded, so I can still write and, with Abby's help, get the paper out on time. Abby, fix coffee. And, when it's ready, we'll boost it from the bourbon bottle. You'll find it in the kitchen on the shelf above the . . . "

"I know where you keep your whiskey," she assured him, making for the kitchen.

"Little Miss Eagle-Eyes," he growled after her. "Larry, Stretch, make yourselves at home and lets chew the fat. We won't make it an interview. I'd as soon socialize with you tearaways."

He made slow work of one-handedly wheeling himself back to his desk and gestured for them to join him there. They drew up chairs, hung their Stetsons and flopped to trade stares with him. He jokingly suggested this was a new and novel experience for them, actually socializing with a professional of a type they usually distrusted.

"We don't mind socializin' with you, Milo," frowned Larry.

"But we don't feel sociable about them that worked you over," muttered Stretch.

"Any idea who?" asked Larry.

"Oh, sure," shrugged Milo. "No doubt in my mind. Unfortunately I was jumped in a dark alley along which I was foolishly taking a short-cut to Main Street, so there's no way I could offer the sheriff or his deputies a description. Didn't see their faces."

"But you know who they are?" prodded Larry.

"In all the time I've run this paper, I've made only one enemy," said Milo. "So they had to be his hirelings. Must've been at least five of 'em. That's really something, huh? Five ganging up on a short-ass like me? And quite a work-over it was. When I went down, two of them used their boots on me. My old pal Doc Parrish had quite a chore that night. They broke my hip as well as the arm. Three ribs damaged. I was delirious for a day and a half. Concussion. But that passed."

"This town has a sheriff with a big reputation," said Larry.

"Since the great Bart Whitney became Sheriff, there's been a drop in the crime rate," Milo said with a wry grin. "For that I give him due credit. Big Bart and his conscientious deputies really are keeping the peace here. It's especially peaceful now that the Dodd-Joel feud has ended. Abby probably told you about that. Well, naturally she's interested. We're personally acquainted with both families. The younger Joel boy has his bachelor eye on her and she'll be one of the Dodd girl's bridesmaids."

"If you got a notion who did this to you, and if you told the sheriff . . ." began Stretch.

"No use confiding my suspicions to Big Bart," said Milo. "As a matter of fact, I've confided in nobody, Just Abby, Doc Parrish and, of course, you two."

"No use tellin' Big Bart?" challenged Larry.

"I ran a story on the Clayton Casino, biggest gambling house in town," explained Milo. "That was after several citizens of my acquaintance complained of being gypped by Billy Clayton's dealers. I printed no accusations of course, merely reported the complaints of my friends. Clayton stormed in here, abused me and warned me never to print such a story again. Well now, maybe you've heard of the Constitution, the right of free speech, freedom of the press . . . "

"We've heard," nodded Larry. "But I want to know why you couldn't rely on the law."

"I'm coming to that," Milo assured him. "As I was saying, Clayton ran off at the mouth. I responded by telling him I'd show no favoritism and would continue to publish opinions as well as facts. A Block D waddy and a storekeeper subsequently claimed they'd been cheated at the casino. I reported their complaints and, that very night, Clayton's men did this to me. Why don't I confide my suspicions to Whitney? Here's why. When Whitney became sheriff, Clayton hailed him as the best thing to happen to Lamont since the coming of the railroad. As a gesture of his esteem, he granted Whitney a twenty-five per cent interest in the casino. Am I claiming the great Big Bart Whitney is now a corrupt official. Certainly not."

"Make up your mind," grouched Stretch, squinting perplexedly. "He draws a percentage of what Clayton's sharpers take from the customers, but he ain't crooked?"

"Clayton's crooked," said Milo. "Whitney's true-blue, above reproach, and living up to his reputation as a lawman of unshakeable courage and integrity."

"You want to make that a little

clearer?" frowned Larry.

"Ever run into Whitney?" asked Milo. The Texans shook their heads. "Wait till you do, size him up, study him a little while and, if you're half as shrewd as you're supposed to be, you'll agree with my opinion of this celebrated defender of the law. Incidentally . . . " He grinned indulgently, "Abby holds to the same opinion. She's nobody's fool, my Abby."

"Did I hear a compliment?" Abby called from the kitchen.

"Fix the coffee — stop snooping!" chided Milo.

"So let's hear it," urged Larry. "How d'you figure Big Bart?"

"Look, I'm not saying he's stupid," muttered Milo. "The man *couldn't* be stupid, could he? I mean, he tamed more towns than Hickok and notched up a big score of convictions, and it's true he's outfought a score or more gunmen who tried to assassinate him. Oh, yes, he's undoubtedly a famous pistolero. But every man has his weakness and I know Whitney's — and Clayton also knows it — and took advantage of it. The simple truth is Whitney's susceptible to flattery. Pat his back, pay him a compliment, mumble a few words of praise — and he's all yours. The man's living off his reputation. He's gotten to where he believes all the far-fetched stories published by fools such as I. In his eyes, Billy Clayton's a successful and reputable businessman and a staunch friend and associate. For Clayton, it was dead easy, a pushover. He treats Whitney as a hero-figure, keeps on heaping praise on him — and Whitney loves him for it."

By the time Abby rejoined them to serve the kind of coffee they most appreciated, Larry was reacting to this revelation in grim amusement. Stretch, a simple soul, was registering shock and sadness.

"It just don't seem decent," he gloomily complained. "It's like spittin' in church or findin' out Robert E. Lee was chicken-livered or Bill Cody can't shoot straight."

"Don't laugh at Stretch," Milo chided his daughter. "Granted some idols have feet of clay, the frontier needs its legends — and Barton Whitney *is* a legend."

"So you won't print nothin' disrespectful about him, huh?" prodded Larry. "About him bein' a sucker for flattery and all?"

"No more than I'd lampoon *your* reputation," declared Milo. "We of the fourth estate have our standards — standards you may never understand."

"How's your coffee?" Abby asked with her bright smile.

Larry took another appreciative swig, returned her smile and assured her,

"You'll hear no complaints from us."

"You gonna do it again, Milo?" frowned Stretch. "I mean get Clayton mad, print about his hired help gyppin' the suckers?"

With Milo's reply, the Texans were

committed. He said it calmly, with no hint of bravado or self-righteousness.

"If I change my policy to please a rogue like Billy Clayton, I'm betraying the profession to which I'm dedicated. I'd never do that."

The Texans traded glances.

"You thinkin' — uh — maybe we'll hang around a while?" prodded Stretch.

"That's what I'm thinkin'," nodded Larry.

"You'll be comfortable at the Hartigan Hotel on Lorring Street," offered Abby. "If Room Five on the first floor is vacant, you should ask for it."

"Tell me why," invited Larry.

"Oh, well . . . " She shrugged casually. "It's a double. Two comfortable beds. And it's a rear room, meaning the window won't give you a view of Lorring Street." She gestured. "Just the alley between Lorring and Main. You'll have a clear view of this building, the back of it."

"Devious little chickadee, aren't you?"

challenged her father. "I'm reading her mind, boys. We're too close to the sheriff's office for Clayton's men to risk a frontal attack — and it might come to that. When Clayton realizes he can't demoralize me, he might just decide to wreck my printing press. That way I'd really be out of business."

"You bluffed us into a promise," Larry reminded Abby.

"I know what you're thinking," she murmured.

"Why do females always say that?" grimaced Stretch.

"You gave your word to visit with Dad and treat him with respect," she conceded. "The promise didn't include any body-guarding chores, any surveillance of our office and home. So you aren't obliged to become our protectors. I can't insist you check into Room Five of the Hartigan, can't force you to have supper with us this evening at six-thirty, can't suggest you risk your spare cash at Clayton's Casino for the sake of sizing up Dad's enemies." She set her cup down and met Larry's intent gaze unflinchingly. "In fact, I can't ask anything more of you. You visited Dad. You've been friendly and respectful, and that's all you agreed to."

"She's so damn devious," remarked Milo, "sometimes it scares me."

"Devious," Larry repeated with a knowing grin. "Uh huh. I'm gettin' to savvy what that word means."

"You and me both," muttered Stretch.

"Of course, if you decide Dad is worthy of your protection, you'll have to stay for the wedding," Abby pointed out. "He'll be a guest and so will most of the casino crowd. I think he'd feel safer with you along. You'd need invitations, but I can arrange that. After all, the bride and groom are both friends of mine."

"In church or in that fine ballroom at the best hotel in town, we'd look like trail-tramps," fretted Stretch.

"Any ideas, Dad?" prodded Abby.

"Funny you should ask," grinned Milo. "There's a local tailor, Barney

Glennis, owes me a favor — a big favor. I think we could make some kind of deal. For instance, if he'll fix you up with the right kind of rigouts, you could return 'em after the festivities, he could brush 'em off and maybe sell 'em."

"After shortening the pants and coats," chuckled Abby. "Not likely Mister Glennis would ever find other customers so tall."

The Texans finished their coffee and got to their feet. As they reached for their hats, Milo mildly enquired.

"What's for supper tonight anyway?"

"Roast beef with all the trimmings," said Abby. "Potatoes and pumpkin and greens and my special gravy. Then peach pie and . . . "

"Runt . . . " Stretch began pleadingly.

"I heard her," nodded Larry. "Stop droolin'." En route to the street-door, he grinned wryly at father and daughter. "We'll come by at six-thirty."

His good humor and Stretch's happy anticipation of a fine supper changed to grim disgust after they quit the *Pioneer* office. Slipping their reins, leading their mounts to the next livery stable south, they traded comments.

"You notice he's a little feller?" scowled Stretch.

"A little hombre and not real strong," Larry said coldly. "Four, maybe five of 'em, worked him over good, left him crippled."

"I call that lowdown," complained Stretch."

"And the hell of it is they got away with it," muttered Larry.

"Don't seem fair, do it?" remarked Stretch. "So — uh — are you thinkin' what I hope you're thinkin'?"

"Well now, we might's well sample the booze at Clayton's Palace," drawled Larry. "And — if there's an empty chair at a poker table . . . "

"Fine by me," shrugged Stretch. "You play poker. I'll watch. Meanin' real careful."

Having surrendered their animals to the care of a stablehand, the tall men toted packrolls, saddlebags and sheathed Winchesters to the Hartigan Hotel on the thoroughfare running parallel with Main. The desk-clerk glanced to the keyrack in response to Larry's request, proffered a key and confirmed Room 5 upstairs was available. They signed the register, paid a week's rent in advance and hefted their gear up the stairs and into the rear double. Larry at once moved to the window to satisfy himself Abby Fenner's sense of direction was reliable.

"How's it look?" asked Stretch, dumping his packroll.

"Looks okay," said Larry. "See a lot of the alley from here and the whole back of the newspaper buildin', the rear door, windows, all of it."

"We're headed for the Palace now, huh?" grinned Stretch.

"After you get one thing straight," cautioned Larry.

"Yeah, what?" demanded Stretch.

"No matter how we hate their guts,

those heroes that beat up on Milo, we ain't about to start a ruckus," stressed Larry.

"Well, like we always say, we never yet started a ruckus," Stretch reminded him. "It's always some hard case starts it."

"But this time is special," declared Larry. "This time it's got to be genuine self-defense. We don't clobber no bastard that ain't tryin' to clobber us and we give 'em first swing."

"Ain't that what we always do?" challenged Stretch. On an afterthought, he added, "And we most always get arrested."

"I'm takin' a chance it won't be just our word against theirs," said Larry. "I mean, if it's the biggest place in town, there'll be plenty other customers. They can't all be close friends of Clayton. So maybe they'll side with us."

"You're gettin' me all mixed up," grouched Stretch. "Are we gonna square accounts for Milo or ain't we?"

"You'd better believe it," growled Larry. "But we got to do it right. And, if Big Bart wants to arrest us, don't smart-talk him, hear? Just follow my lead, do like I do, talk like I talk."

"Been doin' that since way back when we first met up," Stretch pointed out. With an amiable grin and a sly wink, he remarked, "That was many a long year ago, runt, and I ain't complainin'."

"You got faith in me," Larry acknowledged poker-faced. He held a hand to his heart. "And that gets me — right here."

"Think nothin' of it," shrugged Stretch. "We goin' now?"

"Damn right," nodded Larry.

They quit the room, descended to the lobby, surrendered their key to the clerk and moved out into the afternoon sunshine. It took them only a short time to find their way to Lamont's biggest house of entertainment, the gaudy establishment in the heart of town that had become a popular local watering hole and the venue of a fine cross-section of county men, the sporting gentry, local businessmen, off-duty cowhands and the more affluent cattlemen.

Several years had passed since last they had surveyed so spacious an area accommodating games of chance, a dance floor and barroom, the latter dominated by a long, highly polished bar presided over by three brawny dispensers of cheer. There were two platforms strategically located, the larger dais supporting the four chairs occupied by the Palace's musicians, a piano-player, a fiddler, a cornetist and a clarinetist, the smaller one containing a high stool on which squatted an alert-eyed bouncer, a husky character, heavy-featured and seeming in danger of bursting out of his tight-fitting clothes. The place was crowded, but new arrivals, strangers in particular, didn't escape the attention of Clayton's hired women. The Texans were still shouldering their way toward the bar when a satin-gowned bawd appeared at their side, greeting them amiably.

They downed a couple of beers, paid for the bawd's gin, though guessing it to be water, socialized with her for a short time, then made their way to the gambling section. A dapper, impassive houseman, at this moment dealing poker, casually sized them up for a couple of trail-weary no-accounts and nodded to a vacant chair.

"Either of you boys feeling lucky?"

"Not me," said Larry, faking a yawn. "But what the hell? I'll sit in for a hand or two."

He took the empty chair. Stretch found another close by, sagged into it and fished out his makings. So now it began, and they were as ready as they would ever be.

3

Tactical Error

DURING the first two hands, Larry paid attention to his cards and the other players. The good-looking young man at his left waxed sociable and performed introductions. Larry gave his name as Lawrence and learned the houseman was Dan Reeby. The other men, townmen, interested him not at all, but the good-looking young man in the expensive riding clothes rated a sidelong appraisal, having identified himself as Elroy Joel.

Stretch, slumped low in his chair with his Stetson tilted forward, was sizing up the potential opposition from behind a facade of weary indifference. He had already guessed the well-groomed, overweight man with the fake ruby stickpin to be the proprietor, Billy Clayton himself. Clayton was entertaining well-heeled friends at his private table, grinning expansively, ever ready with the quick handshake; in their wanderings the trouble-shooters had encountered many a Billy Clayton.

Stretch covertly appraised the bar-keeps, the bouncer and the impassive supervisors of the roulette, faro and blackjack layouts and wondered how many of them had participated in the brutal beating of the *Pioneer* editor. Any one of them could have beaten hell out of undersize Milo one-handed, but four or more had taken on that easy chore, and probably with relish. Fine heroes. His blood boiled, but his nerve stayed cool.

Patient Larry, observing while not appearing to observe, waited for Reeby's first wrong move and was ready when Reeby made it. The dapper houseman was taking a turn at dealing. Up till now, Larry was a winner, $100 ahead and pretending surprise that Dame

Fortune had so smiled on him. He had created the impression of a not-too-bright trailbum for Reeby's benefit. Reeby was a wily sleight-of-hand artist, he conceded, but over-confident.

"I'd take it kindly," he drawled, "if you'd shuffle and deal again."

The request had the predictably electrifying effect on all parties concerned. The other players, all but Elroy Joel, grimaced uncomfortably and kept their eyes averted. Reeby assumed an expression of polite enquiry. Elroy lit a cigar, glanced sidelong at the impassive Larry, then studied Reeby with keen interest. Stretch nudged his hat up off his brow.

"Something bothering you, cowboy?" drawled Reeby.

"Last card you dealt yourself," said Larry, "didn't come off the top. You slipped it out from under."

"That's how it was," remarked Stretch. "I saw it too."

Reeby's eyes narrowed.

"Are you saddletramps calling me a

cardsharp?" he challenged.

"Maybe you're a sharper, maybe it was just a mistake," shrugged Larry. "Be friendlier to call it a mistake, huh?"

"What do you say to that, Reeby?" smiled Elroy.

"There's been only one mistake here," declared Reeby. "The big feller just made it. I don't appreciate this insult, and Mister Clayton has his own way of dealing with sore losers." He turned in his chair, won the saloon keeper's attention and nodded. "Got a moment, Billy?"

Clayton muttered an apology to his guests, rose and ambled to the table to run a disapproving eye over the Texans and listen to Reeby's complaint. He then nodded impatiently and gave the bouncer a high sign. Big Rufe Gellard promptly quit his stool, bared his teeth in a wolfish grin and flexed his muscles. As if this too were a signal, customers began retreating to neutral vantagepoints.

"You know what to do, Rufe," Clayton said calmly. He beckoned other housemen. "Treen, Hallam, Mole, lend a hand here."

"No need for any rough stuff," frowned Larry.

"We're peaceable, my partner and me," Stretch mildly protested.

"It's just between me and the dealer," Larry pointed out.

"Are you prepared to apologize to Mister Reeby for this insult?" asked Clayton.

"What insult?" Larry raised an eyebrow. "I said he dealt one from under — and he did."

"Sure as hell did," nodded Stretch.

"For that you get thrown out," grinned Clayton.

"Even if we're willin' to walk out quiet?" prodded Larry.

"Saddletramp, you don't get off that easy," said Reeby.

With that, he half-rose, leaned across the table and gave Larry the back of his hand. The other players quickly stood up and stepped clear. Stretch's head then rang from a swinging blow aimed at him from behind; the gambler known as Faro Treen had clobbered him while he was still seated. Wincing, he rose to his full height. So did Larry, loudly announcing.

"Just so everybody understands, this is called self-defense!"

The Texans first retaliatory moves caused a chorus of incredulous gasps, so swiftly did they act. Seized and hurled by Larry, Reeby flew several yards, crashed on face and hands and slid all the way to the front wall, overturning two chairs en route. Simultaneously, Stretch turned on Treen and swung an uppercut that lifted him and flung him against Archer Hallam and Quint Mole, thus temporarily distracting three members of the opposition. Percenters screamed and customers wildly scattered as the mountainous bouncer bore down on Stretch with his arms spread.

Rufe Gellard's attack plan was ill-advised and all too obvious to a veteran brawler of Stretch's calibre — the sudden lunge, the bear-hug imprisoning the victim, crushing mercilessly. Rather than risk such treatment, Stretch slammed three fast ones as soon as Gellard came in range and while his arms were still spread and his mid-section unprotected. He threw everything behind those three fast punches, all the muscle-power his gangling frame belied. Winded, Gellard jerked to a halt. His eyes were glassy, rasping, wheezing sounds erupting from his contorted mouth, as he doubled over. Nimbly, Stretch turned him and swung a hard kick to his backside. The big man lumbered to the bar still in that bent-over posture. His forehead made violent contact with the counter's outer edge and, with an echoing thud, he collapsed and stayed down.

On their feet and rushing Larry, Hallam and Mole ran into trouble. Hallam landed a blow to the side of Larry's head, the only blow he was permitted. Larry didn't reel from it. He stood his ground and gave Hallam a left to the belly and a right that bloodied his nose and sent him hurtling backward to crash onto the poker table and bring it down. When Mole charged, Larry was bending to retrieve his winnings. The casino's roulette supervisor, unable to check his rush, fell across Larry's back. Larry rose and heaved and, when next seen by the bug-eyed onlookers, Mole was somersaulting onto the blackjack table. Lacking the strength to withstand this kind of treatment, the table collapsed.

On his feet again, blood streaming from his mouth, Treen demolished a bottle against the bar and came at Stretch, brandishing its jagged neck-end. Stretch backstepped, allowing him to swing, then grasped the wrist of the hand gripping the bottleneck, also a fistful of Treen's clothing, lifted him shoulder-high and tossed him over the bar. The barkeeps dodged to left and right as the human missile cleared the bartop and crashed against the rear shelves. One of them, the brawny Phil Druce, vaulted the bar, threw himself at Stretch, swung and missed and suffered the same treatment; Treen was rising groggily when Druce's heavy body descended on him.

Reeby, Hallam and Mole, suckers for punishment, were about to resume the attack. As he prepared to defend himself again, Larry called a taunt to the irate Billy Clayton.

"Remember — we offered to go peaceable."

The combined assault of Reeby, Hallam and Mole was as ill-advised as the bouncer's attempt to bear-hug Stretch. After bracing themselves, the Texans stepped forward to meet the onrushing trio. Their left arms came up, blocking wild swings. Their right fists slammed to inviting targets with devastating results. Reeby reeled drunkenly to a street-window, shattering it, pitching through to the sidewalk. The force of Larry's blow drove Hallam all the way to the dais occupied by the musicians. When he flopped unconscious, he pinned the wailing fiddler, plus his instrument.

Infuriated by the applause aimed at the Texans, Mole cursed obscenely, seized a chair and hurled it at Larry. Larry ducked to Stretch's warning yell and, as the chair sped across the barroom, so did everybody else. It hurtled on to demolish a side window, after which Mole took out his frustration on Stretch, or tried to. The vicious kick aimed for the taller Texan's groin swung wide of its mark as Stretch sidestepped and clobbered the kicker. Mole hit the floor shoulder-first, bloody and unconscious.

Came now the impressive entrance of a living legend. With a deputy at his heels, Sheriff Bart Whitney strode majestically into the shambles of shattered glass and wrecked furniture and soreheaded staff-men, came to a halt with feet spread and hands on hips and assumed an expression of official disapproval, thus reducing the uproar of cheering to a subdued muttering.

Eyeing him warily while retrieving their headgear, the trouble-shooters carefully controlled their rarely dormant sense of humor. The shoulder-length hair of the famous towntamer framed a florid visage the most prominent feature of which was a bulbous nose. The bushy brows, flowing mustache and lovingly-tended imperial were a perfect match for the long hair, dark but liberally flecked with grey. The headgear was a snow-white felt hat of the planters style. For afternoon wear, the celebrity favored a black hammertail coat, striped pants tucked into knee-high riding boots with very high heels, white shirt, black string tie and fancy vest. Buckled about the sheriff's considerable midriff was a concho-studded shellbelt with long holsters housing the legendary sidearms, matched Colts, nickel-plated, 7½ inch barrels, ivory-handled.

The staff and clientele allowed Whitney the first word. He studied the scene of chaos through narrowed eys, squared his shoulders and remarked sternly, also unnecessarily, "There has been a disturbance of the peace here."

Slanting his gaze to the onlookers, Larry saw Elroy Joel hide a grin behind his hand. The lugubrious individual standing beside Elroy, lean, black-garbed and sporting a high hat that had seen better days, returned Larry's scrutiny with interest then focused impassively on the great man. Clayton now reappeared, addressing Whitney respectfully and with great warmth.

"Ah, Bart, my friend. I'm grateful you're here. Knew I could count on you."

"Afternoon, Billy." Whitney accorded him an amiable nod. "Got here as fast as I could. Deputy Rockwell noticed one of your tablemen leave the premises through a window, wrecking it in the process, and concluded all was not well here. Passable violent affray, seems like."

"There are your prisoners, Bart,"

announced Clayton, pointing to the Texans. "A sore loser and his sidekick. You know the type. When the luck's against them, they cry cheat and become unruly."

He colored angrily. Having recovered from the impact of Whitney's theatrical arrival, a dozen or more locals began protesting Clayton's accusation. Thus heartened, Larry decided his best chance of staying out of jail was an appeal to the monumental Whitney conceit. He raised his hands to silence the uproar and declared,

"My partner and me sure appreciate you gents speakin' up on our account."

"But all this hollerin' is plumb displeasin' to Sheriff Whitney, I reckon," Stretch joined in. "Let's keep it cool, fellers."

"Damn it, I want these trouble-makers arrested!" raged Clayton.

"Sheriff Whitney, sir, I want to say it's a pleasure and an honor meetin' up with you," drawled Larry, unstrapping his Colt: Stretch was quick to follow his example. "And I know you'd as soon take our statement in your office than listen to all this back-talk in a beat-up saloon."

"A beat-up saloon bein' no place for a famous gent like yourself," nodded Stretch.

"Never was a day us hombres'd irritate the great Bart Whitney," Larry said gravely, proffering his hardware to the frowning deputy.

"Here's mine, Mister Deputy," offered Stretch, passing his sidearms over.

"So we'll come along with you now," nodded Larry.

"Ahem!" The great man cleared his throat and squinted. "Uh — well now . . ."

"You were about to order us along to your office, right Sheriff?" asked Larry.

"At once, yes." Whitney rallied quickly. "Immediately, by Julius!"

"Whatever you say, Sheriff suh," drawled Stretch. "We're with you."

"And maybe some gent, some reliable

witness . . . ?" began Larry.

"My pleasure," said Elroy Joel, stepping forward.

"Guess I'll join you, young Elroy," mumbled the lugubrious one.

About to voice a protest, Clayton grimaced and withdrew a pace. Whitney conveyed on the volunteer witnesses the great honor of an approving nod.

"A son of the reputable Mister Ralph Joel and the always reliable Doc Parrish," he observed. "Ah, yes, your co-operation will be much appreciated." He nudged the deputy. "We'll repair to headquarters now, Matthew."

Deputy Matthew Rockwell, burdened with two extra shellbelts and three extra Colts, signaled the tall men as best he could. They moved out ahead of him with the sheriff following, moving with stately tread, and Elroy and the medico tagging.

En route to the law office, Larry softly remarked to his partner,

"We owe Milo for settin' us straight about Big Bart. This is one time we dodge ten days in a calboose — and it's gonna be dead easy."

"Ain't that the truth," grinned Stretch.

In his office, Whitney hung up his hat and filled the chair behind his desk like a presiding judge. The deputy dumped the Texans' sidearms on the desk, reminded his chief he was on patrol duty and moved out again. The turnkey, a pot-bellied old timer, Tub Jessup by name, puffed on his corncob pipe and loitered by the dealwood door of the ground floor cellblock, ready to take charge of the tall men if so required. Elroy and Parrish helped themselves to chairs. Larry and Stretch won Whitney's approval by staying on their feet, baring their head and studying him admiringly,

"We will begin," Whitney announced, "with your names."

"Lawrence Valentine," said Larry.

"Woodville E. Emerson," offered Stretch. "The E stands for Eustance which I don't never get called, Sheriff Bug-Bit Whitney suh . . . "

"Watch it," chided Larry. "He's Big Bart."

"'Scuse me — Big Bart — slip of the tongue there," the taller Texan apologized. "Mostly I'm called Stretch."

"I never forget a name nor the face that goes with it," Whitney said ponderously. "You are the same Valentine and Emerson better known as the Lone Star Hellions."

"We ain't hellions, heck no," protested Stretch.

"Just a couple travelers cravin' to stay out of trouble," said Larry. "I guess you're wantin' to hear my statement, huh Sheriff? Well, I won't bend your ear more'n a minute. Tinhorn name of Reeby pulled a slick trick which I called him on."

"I saw it too," offered Stretch.

"Slipped himself one from under the deck," explained Larry.

"You'll verify this claim, Mister Joel?" frowned Whitney.

"Sounds unbelievable to me, I'm bound to remark. Fine gentleman like my friend Billy, hardly the kind who'd have a sharper on his payroll."

"I didn't detect the trick-deal," drawled Elroy.

"I didn't either," said Parrish, sighing heavily, stifling a yawn. "Anyway, Valentine's accusation isn't the main issue here, Sheriff. Being a subscriber to the *Pioneer*, I'm as familiar with his reputation as your good self. I naturally anticipated he'd start a brawl, but, to my surprise, he didn't."

"I saw one of my friend Billy's tablemen horizontal on the sidewalk and a lot of broken glass," said Whitney. "I observed further damage within the saloon and several of Billy's other employees in a state of unconsciousness. I also observed . . . "

"I didn't say there wasn't a brawl," shrugged Parrish.

"There surely was a brawl — and it was a beaut," smiled Elroy.

"But Valentine was neither the instigator nor the aggressor," said Parrish. "You concur, young Elroy?"

"Absolutely," nodded Elroy. "The fact is, Sheriff Whitney, both Valentine and his friend attempted to avoid violence when Clayton ordered them thrown out. They offered to leave quietly. I think Valentine's exact words were 'No need for any rough stuff.' But Reeby backhanded Valentine and somebody else struck Emerson . . . "

"Then the rest of Clayton's crew were crowding them," said Parrish. "They were under attack, had no choice but to defend themselves."

"In spectacular style," enthused Elroy.

"Clayton saw the whole thing," the medico assured Whitney. "By the time you arrived, he was in shock I guess, didn't realize what he was saying. In court, I'd have to testify the Texans were set upon and — uh proceeded to resist attack."

"A houseman went at Emerson with a broken bottle — did you notice, Doc?" frowned Elroy.

"I saw it," nodded Parrish. "Very ugly." He shook his head dolefully.

"What some men will do in time of frustration. Very sad. Very ugly."

"I am astounded," said Whitney, who obviously believed his every thought was of vital interest to all. "Knowing you to be honorable men, I am bound to release them."

"We knew you'd treat us square, Sheriff," said Larry. "Guess it's all true what we've heard, huh Stretch?"

"All true," agreed Stretch. "All of it."

"Big Bart gives every man an even break," smiled Larry. "Never plays favorites."

"That's a fact," nodded Stretch.

"This'll be somethin' for us to remember," Larry fervently declared, while Whitney caressed his mustache and nodded condescendingly. "The day we got together with the toughest and squarest badge-toter in the whole damn country."

"Makes a man feel proud," insisted Stretch.

"But, hey now, Big Bart's a busy

man," frowned Larry. "We oughtn't be hangin' around, usin' up his valuable time." He saluted Whitney and reached for his sidearm. "So, if it's all the same to you, Sheriff, we'll get out from under your feet."

"You're free to go," said Whitney. "But it's my duty to warn you, if you mean to stay in this town . . . "

"Hartigan Hotel, Sheriff suh," offered Stretch.

"Room Five," said Larry.

"You know my rules," cautioned Whitney.

"Yes, sir," nodded Larry. "And you can count on us to keep our noses clean."

"We've been called shiftless, but nobody ever took us for fools," said Stretch. "Only a fool'd go up against the one and only Big Butt — 'scuse me — Big Bart Whitney."

"You'll bear that in mind," Whitney said approvingly, as Stretch collected his armory and accorded him a jerky bow.

"Count on it," said Stretch.

"Your co-operation is appreciated, Doc," said Whitney. "Yours too, Mister Joel. You'll convey my respects to your fine parents?"

"Be glad to," grinned Elroy.

Accompanied by Elroy and the medico, the Texans quit the sheriff's office. They strolled a short distance before pausing to strap on their hardware and tie their holster-thongs, also to thank the volunteer witnesses.

"You don't have to thank me," muttered long-faced Parrish. "I've never yet played the games of chance at Clayton's place, which proves how I feel about his hired help." He checked his watch. "Guess I'll look in on friend Milo now, offer him a comprehensive account of that little fracas. He'll be another month of more in that wheelchair, can't get around as fast nowadays." Wistfully, he remarked, "Milo should've been there. It would've warmed his heart, seeing those rogues get their commuppance.

And the look on Billy Clayton's face!"

"Well, Doc, if you're stopping by the newspaper office . . . " began Elroy.

"You don't have to ask," shrugged Parrish. "I'll convey your compliments to Abby."

He nodded to the Texans and ambled away, leaving them to trade appraisals with the younger man. Abby's admirer made no long speech. He only shook hands with the tall men, remarked he had always enjoyed reading of their conflicts with the lawless and expressed the hope they would prolong their stay.

"It's peaceful territory now, what with the feud over and all of us caught up in wedding fever," he assured them. "For your sake, I'm delighted you found Lamont County at this time instead of earlier, when J Bar and Block D were still fighting. A feud is bad business. So many neutrals become involved."

"Well, nothin' like a weddin' to

get the hatchet buried, huh?" prodded Larry.

"My sentiments exactly," said Elroy. "We Joels are reasonable people. My father is a gentleman and Yancy Dodd is a boisterous old firebrand but, despite their contrasting personalities, they're now becoming friends. That water rights dispute was one of those stupid disagreements, the kind that snowballs and starts wars. We're thankful it's all over. Pleasure meeting you gents. I'd best get along to the Savoy. That's where they are now, Dad and old Yancey, conferring with Mayor Lingard about catering for the wedding banquet."

"Sounds a whole lot friendlier'n wranglin' over a doggone waterhole," remarked Stretch.

"And a whole lot easier on Mary Sue and my brother," declared Elroy, as he waved so-long and hurried away.

The Texans steered a course for the Hartigan Hotel, moving stiffly, favoring their strained muscles, feeling at their bruises. Stretch, stealing a glance at his skinned knuckles, quietly declared,

"I'm some happier now."

"That was some helluva hassle," muttered Larry.

"They sure kept us busy," nodded Stretch. "But it was worth the effort, huh?"

"Damn right," nodded Larry. "So now *they* know how it feels. We didn't fit any of 'em for a wheelchair, but they paid for what they did to Milo."

There might be repercussions. They weren't discounting that possibility. But, right now, they thought only of hot baths, the swabbing of their bruised faces and resting of their overworked bodies. For this they had ample time, before taking supper with Milo and daughter.

In the spacious, ornately appointed dining room of Lamont's finest hotel, the ex-hostiles relaxed and lent attentive ears to the talkative owner of the Savoy, Mayor Eugene Lingard. Of an age with the county's two wealthiest cattlemen,

Lingard the visionary was chubby, cheerful and well-groomed, a portly and effusive character with mutton-chop whiskers and a deep conviction that Lamont would eventually become Nebraska's leading city under his administration.

"The wedding party seated at the long table on the dais at the far end," he suggested. "Guests seated at tables lining the walls and the main area reserved for dancing. Of course that will be after the banquet and speeches. It'll be a well-catered affair, I promise you, gentlemen. And no danger the happy couple will miss the midnight train. I've arranged for the driver to convey them to the depot in my own surrey."

"I'm sure Gene will manage everything to our satisfaction, Yancey," smiled Ralph Joel.

"Gene's doin' just fine," agreed Yancey Dodd. "A regular manager from way back, huh Ralph? Any man that can manage his own campaigns and get elected mayor three times runnin', yes siree, he's got to be some manager."

The one-time rival ranchers were a study in contrasts; Joel's younger son was reminded of this when he joined them. His father, tall, distinguished-looking in his town clothes, sensitive-featured and with a mane of greying hair, was the typical gentleman-rancher in every way, unfailingly courteous and of superior intelligence. Ralph Joel was more than a cattleman. Like his brother in St. Louis, he was somewhat more enterprising than the average Nebraska rancher. He believed in capitalising on his excess profits through judicious investment; by this means he had become one of the state's wealthiest citizens.

Cast from a different mold was rough, bow-legged, salty Yancey Dodd, more the old-time cattleman type who had come up the hard way. Of grizzled thatch and blunt, bewhiskered features, he lacked the refinement of his wife, Myra, and her brother Jerome, now a successful and well-to-do lawyer of Denver. Jerome Chadwick had that much in common with Joel and his St Louis brother; his investments assured him an income far in excess of his successful law practice. That bride-to-be, Yancey's beloved daughter, had enjoyed all the advantages of her father's fortune and was every inch as ladylike as her mother. But Yancey would never change. He wore custom-made suits, but not with the aplomb of a Ralph Joel. He owned and drove a surrey as handsome as Joel's, but drove it as though it were a chuck-wagon or a buckboard.

"I'm sure you'll do us proud, Gene," said Joel.

"Just don't forget the eats're on me," growled Yancey. "Me bein' father of the bride, you bill me for this whole spread, savvy?"

"That's understood, Yancey," grinned Lingard.

"And it's agreed all liquor will be paid for by me," Joel reminded them.

"About the booze, Ralph," said Yancey. "We ought to have champagne for drinkin' toasts, huh? Nothin' but the best for the young'uns?"

"The ideal choice, my friend," approved Joel, patting his shoulder.

"Champagne — very appropriate to the occasion," remarked Elroy. "Just as appropriate as the bride's choice of Chicago for the honeymoon, Mister Dodd. Well, Mary Sue always had good taste."

"This smart pup of yours got a real honey-tongue, Ralph," Yancey jovially observed. "Just as smooth a talker as my future son-in-law."

"Happy times, boys," enthused Lingard. "The uniting of two of the county's leading families and the realization of your highest hopes for your children. Max and Mary Sue are a perfect match."

"Compatible," nodded Joel. "Your daughter's a credit to her parents,

Yancey, and may I say Amy and I are delighted."

"Ain't that somethin'?" said Yancey, frowning perplexedly. "All the time we were feudin', your Amy and my Myra were visitin' each other, damned if they weren't, and gettin' along plumb friendly."

"And Max pursued his courtship of Mary Sue," grinned Elroy.

"A man gets so caught up in a fight, he just dunno what's happenin' around him," grouched Yancey.

"The fighting is over, Yancey," declared the mayor. "And that's an advantage to all concerned."

"I certainly have no regrets," said Joel.

"Me now, I got just one regret," confided Yancey.

"Surely not, Mister Dodd," protested Elroy, winking at his father.

"Well, I ain't high-educated like my wife and daughter and you Joels," shrugged Yancey. "Ain't denyin' I'm a rough old cuss . . . "

"More the rough diamond type, my friend," Joel said in his diplomatic way.

"But maybe you can understand my feelin's," muttered Yancey. "Where I grew up, a good weddin' or a good party meant a good fight. Somebody always got to scrappin' and nobody minded. Sheriff pretended like he didn't see — or maybe he was too drunk to notice. Wouldn't matter who got to swingin' punches. Everybody'd gather round and cheer, the bride and groom and their folks, the preacher."

"An interesting tradition," Elroy commented poker-faced.

"The good grub, the booze and the dancin' were fine," Yancey sentimentally recalled. "But what really rounded it off and got the young'uns started on their married life was the fightin'. I remember how it was when Myra and me got hitched in Omaha. Doggone, that was a long time back. Omaha wasn't like you see it now."

"I'm sure it was a happy function

— following a beautiful ceremony," said Joel.

"Everybody had a time," sighed Yancey. "There were these three jaspers started a ruckus while Myra's old man — may he rest in peace — was makin' his speech. These jaspers that was fightin' didn't even have invites to the shindig. Well, that made Myra's pa good and mad and my old Uncle Luke didn't take kindly to it neither. So they quit speech-makin' a while and got into the fight and I got into it too. It bein' a sociable occasion, five or six other fellers joined in." He grinned reminiscently. "Real fine fight. I ended up with a black eye, but Myra forgave me. Mighty understandin' woman, my Myra."

"Other times," Elroy said sympathetically.

"*Better* times," insisted Yancey.

In cities to the southeast and southwest of Lamont, this same afternoon, relatives of the Dodds and Joels discussed the coming wedding. Having accepted invitations to attend, they now expressed hope this happy occasion would be unmarred by violence. Unlike Yancey Dodd, the Joels of St Louis and the Chadwicks of Denver keenly disapproved of unseemly behaviour at social functions.

Of course none of these genteel folk had any clear notion of what was in store for them.

4

A Better Class Of Wedding Guest

BEING the finest restaurant in St. Louis, the Cafe de Paris would have assured its owner of a handsome income. The venue of the big city's upper crust was an impressive triple-storey edifice in the best part of town with the lush living quarters of the Joel family located on its top floor. But Lester Joel was as astute an investor as his gentleman-rancher brother, and so his fortune had increased year by year.

Two years Ralph's junior, every inch as handsome and distinguished, he took coffee with his dark-haired, well-corseted spouse in their parlor at about the same time Mayor Lingard was in discussion with the fathers of the bride and groom. Stella Joel, never having ventured west of St. Louis, was apprehensive but determined to make an impression on the other guests.

"I abhor the prospect of traveling to so primitive an outpost," she declared. "But we Joels will be well to the fore, I promise you, Lester. I'll not be upstaged by Myra Dodd's high and mighty sister-in-law at this or any other function."

"Now, Stella," Lester said soothingly. "I doubt the Chadwicks have any intention of showing off. He's a successful attorney after all and quite well-to-do. As for Hildegard Chadwick, I can't imagine she'd try to upstage you."

"Well-to-do is an understatement," she retorted. "If Jerome Chadwick could afford to present his wife with the Kuruman diamond — of all things — for a wedding anniversary gift . . . "

"A beautiful piece, I'm sure," he shrugged. "But you should worry? Wearing your ruby pendant, you'll be as dazzling a vision as Hildegard Chadwick — always assuming she'll wear the diamond."

"As if she'd miss the opportunity," sniffed Stella.

"And Lamont is by no means primitive," he hastened to assure her. "Just a few days ago, when Dexter Dyson was lunching here, he spoke of the place. Apparently he passed through there en route to Seattle quite recently. Most favorably impressed. Quite a frontier metropolis, he said."

"I live in hopes," said Stella.

She sipped coffee, cocked an ear and winced. Lester shrugged resignedly. From the next room, the sound produced by their daughter at piano practice tended to grate on the ears. Not that 21-year-old Claudette Joel had a heavy hand. On the contrary, her keyboard technique was as tentative, as gentle, as devoid of assurance as her reticent self. Painfully, shy, Claudette was the despair of her mother.

"This is cruelty, my dear," Lester

quietly protested. "Poor Claudette. After so many years of personal tuition from the best music teachers, she still has no ear, no sense of timing, no aptitude at all. Shouldn't we put her out of her misery? Must she practice — when it's so obviously futile?"

"The music lessons are part of my grand plan," said Stella, shrugging helplessly. "The good Lord knows I've tried, Lester. Oh *how* I've tried!"

"I too," he nodded. "But shouldn't we resign ourselves to the sorry truth? The child simply lacks confidence."

"She is no longer a child," fretted Stella. In exasperation, she called to her daughter. "Claudette! Enough!"

"And we share the same fear, I know," frowned Lester. "Will she never attract a suitable marriage prospect? Will we never get her off our hands?"

"You have to admit that's a gruesome thought," insisted Stella.

"Well, I wouldn't say gruesome," he protested.

"*I* would," Stella said vehemently.

"When we're out together, I just know what people are thinking. How could Stella Joel, wife of the handsome proprietor of the Cafe de Paris, be mother to such a wallflower?"

"Claudette has her good points," he suggested.

"I'm not worrying about her appearance, Lester," said Stella. "She's presentable enough — but so gauche, so utterly devoid of personality, so depressingly self-conscious."

"Too confined," opined Lester. "The trip will do wonders for her."

"You hope," sighed Stella.

"Well, I mean, a broadening experience," he suggested. "We've never traveled so far before. When we last visited Ralph, it was in Springfield, Illinois, remember? I'm looking forward to seeing his Nebraska holdings and I'm sure Claudette will enjoy herself."

"Lester, she *never* enjoys herself — *anywhere*," complained Stella.

"How does she feel about the trip?" he asked.

"I havent mustered the courage to tell her," said Stella. "I can't bear to see her flinch. And she'll flinch, you may be sure."

"We can't delay it any longer," he frowned. "After all, my dear, we're leaving tomorrow afternoon. She needs time to pack."

Stella set her empty cup down, eyed her husband challengingly and insisted,

"*You* call her in — *you* tell her."

"It has to be done," declared Lester.

And so he called his daughter into the parlor and, with many an encouraging smile, told her of the Lamont wedding and the family's proposed attendance at same. Claudette was the same height as her mother, 5 feet 6, and as attractive as Stella had been at age 21, but nowhere as compelling a personality. She stood there with hands clasped in front of her, garbed in a gown created by St Louis' foremost fashion designer, dark-haired, of good complexion and figure, a pretty woman who rarely rated a second glance from the opposite sex thanks to her shyness.

"She's flinching — see?" sighed Stella.

"Stop flinching, Claudette," Lester gently chided. "There is no need to flinch."

"Yes, Papa," Claudette said nervously. "Will this mean — I'll have to meet people — talk to people?"

"Give me strength!" groaned Stella.

"Steady, my dear," frowned Lester. "Claudette, my pretty dove, of course you'll meet and talk to people, but is that such an ordeal? They'll be our relatives, new friends, pleasant frontier folk who — uh — who'll take you to their hearts. My little princess will charm them, I know."

"You know that's not so, Papa," mumbled Claudette.

"In Lamont, Nebraska, you'll blossom," Lester bravely predicted. "You'll be as attractive as any woman there. You dance well. You'll be admired, sought after . . . "

"Stop *dreaming*, Lester!" snapped Stella.

"Now, Stella . . . " began Lester.

"No, Mama's right," Claudette declared with uncharacteristic vehemence. "It's no use, Papa. I'm a lost cause. I can't make clever conversation. I'll never learn to play the piano — and I feel so *guilty* about that . . . "

"Your father and I have decided your music lessons will be discontinued," Stella said irritably. "You won't be expected to practice any more."

"Thank you, Mama, oh, thank you!" gasped Claudette. To the consternation of both parents, she stumbled to Stella's chair and flung her arms about her. "You're so terribly kind and I'm such a disappointment to you and — and you deserve so much better after all you've done for me . . . !"

"You're choking me," protested Stella. "and disturbing my coiffure."

" . . . and I'll try harder, honestly," promised Claudette. "I'll really try to — to please you this time. I'll force myself to smile as often as you want me to and to be socially acceptable to Uncle Ralph and Aunt Amy and — and say all the right things."

"Don't distress yourself, Claudette," muttered Lester.

"Young ladies of good background do not display their emotions, even in the privacy of their parents' parlors," chided Stella. She extricated herself from her daughter's impulsive embrace, but gently, softening a little. "Claudette, dear Claudette, I'll not hold you to that rash promise, but I do appreciate your good intentions. Mother knows you mean what you say. I have been disappointed, that's true, but stop worrying now. Just do your best and remember Papa and I don't expect miracles."

"I'll go pack now," murmured Claudette, backing away from her. "And I really *will* try, Mama. I'll make you proud of me yet."

After his daughter had left them, Lester smiled placatingly.

"You see, dear? She really is trying."

"*Terribly* trying," complained Stella. "But of course I'll never abandon her. She's still my flesh and blood, the child I bore — though sometimes I wonder about that."

"Do you suppose . . . ?" Lester grimaced uneasily, "a mistake of some kind at the hospital — after the birth . . . ?"

"I went back to the hospital with Doctor Pascal and demanded an investigation," she grimly assured him.

"You did?" he blinked.

"Several years ago," she nodded.

"And . . . ?"

"No mistake. The old records were checked. There were only two births at Saint Joan's that day. Claudette was born at ten in the morning. They brought her to me at noon, as I recall. The other babe arrived much later, nine-thirty p.m."

"I shouldn't have asked. She's undoubtedly our child, Stella!"

"And maternal instincts prevail," said

Stella. "I'll never disown her, Lester. But oh how I pray she'll break free of her shell and become confident and poised! That's what she needs, Lester. Poise, assurance, aplomb."

"It could happen," offered Lester.

"I'll continue to pray," said Stella.

* * *

Jerome Chadwick left the Central Court of Denver at 3 p.m. that day and, some thirty minutes later, was relaxing with his Philadelphia-born wife on the terrace of their fine home in the big town's most exclusive residential sector. The only case demanding his personal attention, an action for slander, had been successfully concluded.

"Judge Hardacre was less long-winded this time, I'm thankful to say," he reported.

"He found in favor of your client?" asked the fair Hildegard.

"And awarded heavy damages," smiled Jerome. "The fee will be substantial.

Oh, yes. Quite substantial."

"How nice," she murmured.

"No urgent cases pending at this time," he drawled. "With Wilbur in charge at the office, I can easily spare time for our visit to Lamont." He smiled affectionately at his stately spouse as he lit a Havana cigar. Denver's wealthiest attorney was in his mid-40's, an impressive if not handsome man. Of compact physique, he was urbane, astute and supremely content. His finances were secure and his wife the reigning beauty of Denver's high society; what more could a man ask of life? "We deserve this little diversion, Hildegard. The children are fully occupied with their studies at Sacramento College and the servants can be relied upon to take care of the house in our absence, so we're free, my dear, for a week or more. It will be like a second honeymoon."

Cool and poised at all times, regal in her demeanor, the lawyer's wife returned his smile, but confided misgivings.

"Such a pity it has to be a town like Lamont, a thriving cattle centre," she remarked. "Dusty and noisy, I imagine, with a great many ruffianly inhabitants."

"I felt bound to accept the invitation," he pointed out.

"Yes, you're quite fond of the bride-to-be, your sister's child, and who could blame you?" she smiled. "Mary Sue. Such a sweet girl."

"Still a strong bond between us, Myra and me," he reminded her. "Old Yancey, I'm sure, will be as rough as ever, but he's a good man at heart, you know. Devoted husband and father . . . "

"You don't have to apologize for your brother-in-law," said Hildegard. "I can cope with him. It's Lamont itself that alarms me, and the prospect of rubbing shoulders with the hoi polloi."

"I can reassure you in that regard," said Jerome. "Just yesterday, I received a reply to my letter to the mayor, fellow name of Lingard. He writes well, obviously a gentleman of good background."

"But, as mayor of Lamont, he'd surely paint a rosy picture of the place," she suggested.

"I believe he's been frank with me," said Jerome. "And I must say I'm favorably impressed. The town really is progressing under his administration. The chief law officer, for instance, is the illustrious Barton Whitney. Veteran lawman, you know, the kind who strikes fear into the hearts of roughnecks and criminals. There has been a marked decline in rowdyism, Mayor Lingard assures me, so I doubt we'll be subjected to any embarrassing incidents. Anyway, we'll be guests at Block D, so you'll be well-protected. The ranch has been improved over the years, Myra said in her last letter. Fine furnishing, ample accommodation, no shortage of servants. We'll be very comfortable there, I'm sure."

"We'll not disappoint Myra," she

promised. "I do realise how much our visit means to her."

"And to me," he said wistfully. "Family reunions are always a pleasure, It will be good to see Myra again and, of course, meet the bridegroom's family. Myra speaks highly of the Joels."

"Early departure tomorrow," she said ruefully.

"But the train journey will be comfortable," he predicted. "I've reserved a private compartment for us."

"You'll wire your sister before we leave?" she pleaded. "I'd feel less nervous, I'm sure, if we were met at the Lamont depot immediately we arrived."

"It will be quite a reception," he grinned. "The family surrey to transport us to Yancey's ranch, probably a wagon for our baggage and an escort of Block D riders. They'll do us proud, Hildegard, never fear." He hesitated a long moment before asking, "Have you had second thoughts about our little treasure?"

"No second thoughts," said Hildegard. "It's a special occasion after all, so why shouldn't I wear the Kuruman?"

"Mary Sue would be flattered," he opined. "She'd regard it as a compliment, a grand gesture on your part. And a happy omen. Anyway . . . " He reached for her hand and squeezed it. "We know the diamond will be safe, don't we?"

Hildegard Chadwick chuckled huskily as she rose to her feet. She was tall and fine-figured, her beauty unimpaired by motherhood and the passing of the years.

"Must finish our packing now," she murmured. "Yes, the Kuruman diamond will be safe. Only you and I know *how* safe, right, Jerry darling?"

"Right," nodded her admiring husband.

* * *

That evening, while Larry and Stretch socialized with Milo Fenner and daughter over supper, the owner of the Clayton Casino dined in his private quarters and conferred with his chief henchman. The sardonic Archer Hallam had bathed and changed after participating in the afternoon's memorable fracas, but still appeared much the worse for wear, his scars and bruises very much in evidence, his mood resentful. He swigged bourbon while watching Clayton eat.

"We got the smashed windows boarded up and the broken glass cleared away, but the place is a mess, a damn shambles," he sourly complained. "And the hell of it is those saddlebums are walking free. Why in blazes didn't Whitney lock 'em up?"

"He came by to talk with me an hour ago," muttered Clayton.

"Are we gonna have trouble with that bonehead?" scowled Hallam.

"I can handle Whitney," Clayton assured him. "Damn it, Arch, all it takes is a pat on the back and a compliment or two. He'll believe anything I tell him."

"And you told him . . . ?"

"The whole thing was the result of a misunderstanding. Don't worry. He bought it."

"Yeah, fine, but maybe the reputation of the casino will suffer, Billy. This place is a bonanza — as long as the suckers keep coming back for more. We have heavy expenses. We can't afford a drop in our profits."

"Arch, compared with what I'm planning, our take from this place is nickels and dimes." Clayton said that softly and with his eyes gleaming. "We'll be able to sell out and quit, turn our backs on Lamont and never scramble for a buck as long as we live. One big take. That's what counts, Arch. And we could pull it off."

Hallam promptly forgot his aches and pains and frustrations.

"Just what've you got in mind?"

"When I first read of it, I cut the whole half-page out of a Denver paper," said Clayton. "That was — hell — must've been near a year ago. Sometimes something leaves a lasting impression, know what I mean? This was one of those times." He downed another mouthful and rose from his chair. "It's still here somewhere." Temporarily abandoning his meal, he rummaged in a drawer of the dresser. The clipping was brought to light and passed to Hallam. "Go ahead. Read that. Then I'll make your mouth water, I promise you."

Under the column heading: DENVER LAWYER BUYS KURUMAN DIAMOND — RECORD PRICE Hallam studied photographs of Colorado's most well-known attorney and his strikingly beautiful wife. He then read the report of Jerome Chadwick's acquisition of the South African gem believed to be equal in value to the fabulous Kohinoor diamond of India.

"Wedding anniversary gift for his

wife," he observed. "Some gift."

"And negotiable," grinned Clayton, resuming his meal. "Anywhere in 'Frisco or along the east coast, there'll be interested parties who'd pay a fortune to get their paws on the Kuruman. To meet our price, they'd probably form a combine, pool all their ready cash."

"I'm too well known in Denver," warned Hallam. He finished his reading of the report and shook his head emphatically. "No way I'd risk being recognized by a Colorado lawman."

"You and Faro are the smartest thieves on my team," Clayton mumbled while munching. "But that doesn't mean I plan on taking the whole outfit to Denver for a raid on the Chadwick home. Not so you'd notice, Arch. Not necessary anyway. We don't have to go to the diamond. It's coming our way, and soon."

"This bauble's gonna be right here in Lamont?" frowned Hallam. "How do you know that?"

"You haven't been reading the social news in Fenner's paper," said Clayton. "Who do you suppose Chadwick is? Just Myra Dodd's brother. How about that? The Chadwicks are coming to Lamont for the wedding — and do you suppose Hildegard Chadwick'd pass up this chance to show off the Kuruman? The Joel's have high-toned kinfolk too, Joel's brother from Saint Louis. It's gonna be a very swank affair, Arch. And don't forget we're on the guest list, you, me, Faro and Rufe. Lucky for us, huh? Just like Ralph Joel to ask me to bring Rufe along. The Joels are leery of rowdiness. To make sure no booze-blind guests get out of hand, Rufe'll be there to remove 'em from the scene." He chuckled softly. "Discreetly, of course."

"You figure that's the best time for grabbing the diamond?" prodded Hallam.

"Listen, there's bound to be some kind of disturbance," insisted Clayton. "In a big gathering, any kind of ruckus spreads like wildfire. That's what old Yancey Dodd's hoping for — a little excitement to liven up the proceedings."

"Sounds good," nodded Hallam. "All it takes is for one or both of us to be close to the Chadwick woman — waiting our chance."

"The Kuruman is gonna be ours and that's a fact," Clayton said bluntly. "But, between now and the big shindig, we don't talk of it except in private. No need to explain the deal to Faro or Rufe this soon. The wedding day will be time enough."

"Then it'll be goodbye Nebraska and hallo New York," enthused Hallam. "You're right, Billy. This'll be the big one."

"Suit you?" grinned Clayton.

"Damn right," declared Hallam. "I always did plan on retiring early. Why wait till I'm too old to enjoy what's mine?"

* * *

Partaking of the very satisfying supper dished up by their hostess, the Texans relaxed and waxed amiable. How often had they accepted the hospitality of — of all people — a newspaper editor? Their memories were dim on that question. But, as Larry had often remarked, there has to be a first time for everything. Newspaperman or not, Milo had what it took to win their admiration and support. The *Pioneer*'s frail founder-editor was revealed as a man of indomitable spirit and unchallengable integrity. He had suffered at the hands of thugs who had been punished for so brutally assaulting him. He was still experiencing pain and would be partially incapacitated for some time to come. Despite this, he wasn't about to let up on a sharper cunningly camouflaged as the proprietor of a reputable gambling house.

"Rogues like Clayton give me a severe pain in the ass," he confided, while his daughter withdrew to the kitchen to pour coffee. "I figure this is something I have in common with you fiddlefoots. Admit it, Larry. You and Stretch are compulsive gamblers. On the frontier, damn near all men gamble at some time or other. I'm not opposed to gambling any more than I'm opposed to hard liquor. If a man wants to risk his cash in a game of chance, that's his privilege. But, damn it, he rates an even chance, right? In gambling, that's the prime factor."

"An even chance is all we ever look for," nodded Larry.

"Cardsharps." Milo grimaced in disgust and, confident Abby was out of earshot, expressed that disgust in some imaginative cussing. "No better than horse-thieves or rustlers, you agree? And the worst of the breed are scum like Billy Clayton, the kind who train and pay a whole staff of double-dealing tinhorns."

"So you ain't lettin' up on 'em," guessed Stretch.

"Bet your Texas spurs, boy," growled

Milo. "I'm staying after Clayton until Bart Whitney finally gets wise." With a genial grin, he added, "That's why I'm pleased you're renting Room Five at the Hartigan."

Abby rejoined them, distributed coffee and flashed Larry an impish grin.

"Well, Mister Trouble-Shooter? Are all newspapermen alike, one no better than the others?"

"You win, Abby," he shrugged. "Ain't much of your pa . . . "

"And what there is is plumb toil-worn," said Stretch.

" . . . but he's a scrapper," Larry conceded. "And, like he says, we do see eye to eye, at least about Clayton."

"Got to admit I feel a little guilty," she murmured, her smile fading.

"About what, honey?" demanded her father.

"You mean it hasn't occurred to you?" she asked. "I took advantage of them by the North Loup, tricked them into coming to Lamont."

"Sure you did," shrugged Milo. "So?

You hear them complain?"

"Look at their faces," she frowned. "Can we pretend we aren't responsible?"

"Forget it," said Larry. "Stoppin' by the casino was our own idea."

"You wouldn't have talked of that fight," guessed Milo. "Well, you didn't need to. My friend Doc Parrish warmed my heart with a graphic account of the whole hullabaloo."

"Larry Valentine, you did it deliberately," accused Abby. "You went to Clayton's hoping for an excuse to black a few eyes and break a few jaws."

"Wouldn't have laid a fist on any of 'em, if they hadn't started pushin' us around," Stretch mildly protested. "Shucks, Abby, all we did was defend ourselves."

"I still feel bad about it even if Dad doesn't," said Abby. "I'd have been grateful enough for having you watch our back door nights, kind of bodyguarding Dad. I didn't mean for you to punish the men who hurt him.

That's exactly what you did, isn't it? And you could've ended up in jail."

"No danger of that," argued Milo. "Not with Doc supporting their self-defense claim."

"We're obliged to young Elroy too," remarked Larry.

"Nice feller," grinned Stretch.

"I approve of him," said Milo. "Abby insists he's too sure of himself."

"I'm not ready to be courted anyway," said Abby. "Got my hands full taking care of my crusading dad who keeps forgetting how old he is — and how puny."

"It's not muscle that counts — it's what's in here," Milo retorted, raising a finger to his temple. "You think it's muscle and fast shooting that keep these tearways alive and more than a match for the outlaws they fight? Guess again, child of mine. It's brain-work, savvy, cunning, fast thinking when the chips are down." He grinned blandly at his guests. "You see? No matter what your attitude toward newspapermen, you can't deny we have plenty in common."

"Have it your way — scribbler," shrugged Larry.

"Now that you've met the great Bart Whitney, do you go along with our opinion?" asked Abby.

"He's something else," chuckled Stretch. "Hey, you should've heard Larry flim-flam him."

"Doc told me," nodded Milo. He finished his coffee, lit a cigar and held forth a while on the subject of legends. "A brave man, Whitney, and incorruptible. Dedicated too. A credit to the profession of law enforcement, but guillible. Pity the celebrity who begins believing his own publicity. He is similar in many ways to Bill Cody. Now Cody is undoubtedly a genuine hero, but did he perform all the daring deeds described by Buntline . . . ?"

"By who?" asked Larry.

"Ned Buntline, a dime novelist, a bunko man with an eye to the main chance," Milo said disdainfully.

"Believe what Buntline has written of Cody and you'll believe Buffalo Bill is superhuman."

"We ain't much for readin'," shrugged Stretch.

"The same Buntline has written several potboilers with Whitney as his hero," explained Milo. "Now it's Whitney getting the treatment, lurid, flamboyant prose, grossly exaggerated if not completely imaginary. Fiction! Lies!"

"Book-writers must be a plumb peculiar bunch," frowned Stretch.

"Need I add Whitney is delighted?" grouched Milo, "It's obvious he's convinced himself it's all true. He *wants* to believe all that hogwash, so he *does*."

"So now you know," said Larry.

"Now I know what?" asked Milo, eyeing him warily.

Abby winked knowingly at Stretch, who grinned and looked away.

"Now you know why the beanpole and me don't believe half of what you scribblers print about us," Larry said relentlessly. "If we believed it, if we fooled ourselves like Big Bart fools himself, we'd have gotten our heads blowed off years ago."

"Ain't that the truth," agreed Stretch. "We'd think we're bullet-proof, which no man is."

Milo sighed heavily.

"Touche," he said. "In spades."

The newpaperman, his daughter and their guests changed the subject. The coming marriage of Max Joel and Mary Sue Dodd was now discussed while, in the North Kansas township of Tyson, a stopover on the state route, two professional assassins made ready to earn their fee.

Cordeau and Barris had reached Tyson an hour before the arrival of the northbound stage. Identifying their intended victim had been ridiculously easy; Barris had tagged the passengers to the Garland Hotel and watched unsuspecting George Middleton sign the register. He had also ascertained the location of George's overnight accommodation, Room 9 on second floor, after which he and Cordeau had rented a double on the same floor.

When, after supper, George decided to take a walk along Tyson's main stem, the killers followed, but cautiously, hugging the unlit areas, keeping him in sight, waiting their chance.

The young cashier was crossing the street, moving toward the Silver Stirrup Saloon, an inviting target, when Cordeau and Barris slunk into an alleymouth. There, Cordeau drew and docked a Smith & Wesson .38 and took aim while his partner grinned callously. Under these conditions, how could a back-shooter miss?

5

. . . Try, Try Again

IT had happened before and, undoubtedly, would happen again. It was not the first time George Middleton had tripped on the edge of a sidewalk and measured his length, but this time was different, a lucky time for him.

He was clearly silhouetted against the brightly-lit street window of the saloon in the instant before Cordeau squeezed trigger. Then his boot caught the edge of the sidewalk and he was sprawling, the evening air blasted by the gunshot and the .38 slug cutting through the space occupied by his body a moment before, speeding on to shatter the window and a tankard of beer, the handle of the latter being held by a drinker at the Silver Stirrup bar.

Along the street, shouts were raised. Locals were converging on the scene and, loath to risk a second shot under these circumstances, Cordeau returned his pistol to its shoulder-holster, nudged Barris, turned and took to his heels.

"I'll mangle the sonofabitch that did this!" Town marshal Abe Armstrong vowed at the top of his voice. "Let's go, Clem! Let's nail the bastard!"

There was of course, ample justification for the burly lawman's mounting rage. To be raising a jug and voicing a toast to Deputy Clem Danford on the occasion of the third anniversary of Danford's appointment as his deputy, to have that almost full tankard shattered by a bullet, was more than a shock. It was an embarrassment. And Abe Armstrong did not take kindly to embarrassment. With his shirtfront beer-saturated and festooned with slivers of glass, scrawny Danford was almost as embarrassed, and certainly as irate as his boss.

"Everybody stay put!" ordered

Armstrong, not that any of the saloon's staff or clientele relished the notion of barging outside in search of some trigger-happy jackass discharging a pistol at lighted windows.

The marshal and his deputy erupted from the saloon entrance as a couple of raging avengers to descend on the stranger picking himself up from the sidewalk.

"Gotcha!" roared Armstrong.

"I got him too!" gasped Danford, imprisoning George's right arm. "Don't let go — for gosh sakes — till I disarm him!"

"What's happening?" cried George. "Unhand me please!"

"Hark at him," sneered Armstrong, with an arm locked about George's neck. "Unhand me he says — innocent as you please — and right after shootin' a beer outa my hand."

"Shoot? I don't shoot!" protested George. "I mean — I'm unarmed. I carry no weapon."

"How'd you get rid of the hogleg?"

demanded Danford.

"The what?"

"The pistol! Where'd you stash it, Mister Sharpshooter?"

"I don't know what you're talking about. I own no pistol, carry no pistol. I'm nervous of firearms, don't even touch the bank revolver under my cash drawer — back at the Reliance Bank."

Having gotten well clear of the scene, Cordeau was planning his next move.

"We have to make provision for further reversals," he muttered to Barris. "The night's still young. We could still take care of him here, but maybe not. So, as a precaution, you'd best hustle along to the stage depot. If they have room for us, buy a couple tickets. Then meet me in the lobby of the Garland."

By now, the hapless George was firmly planted in a chair in Armstrong's musty-smelling office and undergoing intense interrogation; some time after the turn of the century, the procedure would be termed the third degree by police and prisoners alike. A half-dozen townmen had been recruited to the task of searching the whole area in front of the Silver Stirrup for a thrown-away handgun of unknown calibre. While Armstrong bellowed accusations at the supposed culprit, Danford hovered beside his boss and picked his teeth. Somebody had once told him this gave him a fiendish look, baring his teeth, jabbing at them with a toothpick; he was counting on this routine to spook the captive into a confession.

"I would like to help," George declared, when Armstrong paused to catch his breath. "I have great respect for officers of the law and have always co-operated with them as best I could. I am a law-abiding citizen who wouldn't dream of discharging a firearm at a peace officer. This is a ridiculous situation."

"Real sneaky character, Abe," warned Danford. "Real cool. Gonna be a hard one to crack."

"Law-abidin' citizen," jeered Armstrong.

"Sheriff Phelan of Shadlow County will vouch for my good reputation," offered George.

"What'd he say?" frowned Danford.

"Howzat again?" challenged Armstrong.

"I am well known to the law authorities of my hometown — Shadlow, Kansas," said George. "As a matter of fact, I'm to be witness for the prosecution in a murder case to be held on the twenty-fifth. Meanwhile I'm traveling to Lamont, Nebraska, to attend a wedding. I can show you the invitation and, of course, you'll wire Sheriff Phelan for confirmation of my bona fides."

He fished out his invitation. Armstrong inspected it, gnashed his teeth and ordered Danford to telegraph the Shadlow sheriff. The deputy was halfway to the door when Armstrong changed his mind.

"Hold it, Clem. I ain't so sure now."

"You believin' this jasper?" prodded Danford.

"Maybe he could do it, but I got my doubts," grouched Armstrong. He checked his vest pockets, found half of a stogie, clamped it between his teeth and scratched a match for it. Through the smoke-haze, he studied George intently. "So what d'you know about the shootin'? You were right there in front of the saloon, damn it. You must've seen *somethin'*."

"I can be of little help," George said sheepishly. "All I can tell you is I was crossing toward the saloon with the intention of partaking of a modest libation before retiring. I did hear the shot, yes . . . "

"Where?"

"From somewhere behind me. But then I tripped and fell."

"You always a tanglefoot — got some kinda problem, son?"

"I am clumsy, yes. Doctor Everly in Shadlow calls it an interesting condition." George sighed wistfully.

"I'm glad he finds it interesting. To me it's a constant embarrassment. I stumble frequently — too frequently — and I lack manual dexterity. I manage fairly well at the bank. I'm junior cashier at the Reliance Bank of Shadlow. Counting out cash, making accurate tallies of deposits and withdrawals, that's no problem at all, but in other ways, I'm just naturally awkward."

"That all he's gonna tell us?" asked Danford.

"The shot and my fall, the sound of breaking glass, seemed to happen at the same time," shrugged George. "That's really all I can tell you. But, please, if you're disinclined to believe me, wire Sheriff Phelan."

"I don't reckon we'll be wirin' the Shadlow sheriff," said Armstrong. "Plain enough, Clem. Some joker got booze-blind and cut loose with a six-shooter, likely didn't even see young Middleton. Crazy accident, the slug hittin' my beer. Then the joker spooked and skedaddled."

"So maybe we'll never know," complained Danford.

"Well," scowled Armstrong, "if I ever get my hand on him — specially his neck . . . "

A few minutes later, freed by the local law authorities, a somewhat shaken George Middleton made his way back to the Garland Hotel. The after-supper stroll had been ill-advised, he reflected. It didn't seem a dangerous notion at the time he left the hotel, just a leisurely stroll along the main street, just stopping by some friendly saloon for just one short shot of whiskey before retiring. He was moderate in his habits, never drank to excess. Come to think of it, the Garland had its own bar, so he would now have that much-needed nightcap.

To his surprise, a couple of strangers, well-groomed and courteous, confronted him the moment he entered the lobby. They at once waxed solicitous, commenting on his pallor, his obvious state of shock.

"What you need, my young friend, is a little something to brace your nerves," said Cordeau, taking his arm. "Calvin's the name. This is my friend, Mister Barlow. And you?"

"George Middleton. This is very kind of you."

"Some disagreeable experience perhaps?" enquired Barris.

"Very much so, Mister Barlow," nodded George, as they escorted him into the bar. "The marshal has decided it must have been an inebriated gunman who fired a shot and smashed a window. He at first suspected me."

"The nerve of the marshal, jumping to such a conclusion," drawled Cordeau. "He should know better than to accuse a gentleman of your calibre."

"Most kind of you to say so," George acknowledged.

"Not at all," smiled Cordeau. "Let's take that vacant table. Mister Barlow, you'll take care of the drinks?"

"Be glad to," said Barris. "What's your pleasure, Mister Middleton?"

"Just a small whiskey, if you please," said George. "Rye would do nicely."

"Same for us," said Cordeau.

The professionals did not always rely on well-aimed bullet or a thin-bladed knife for their homicidal purposes; there had been no inquests on several of their victims. The powder dropped into one of the three shot glasses by Barris was a slow-acting poison devised by the wily Cordeau. The victim invariably died in his sleep of apparent heart failure.

To the table where Cordeau and the intended victim sat, Barris carried the three glasses, taking care to set the spiked rye before the intended victim. He seated himself and what followed caused the killers to trade startled glances. George began moving glasses on the table top in pretty much the same way a grifter arranges and rearranges the cup concealing the pea in the shell game, moving them in circles that bewildered his chagrined hosts, and with a quite deft action. How could they be sure which glass contained the lethal shot?

"Excuse me," he smiled. "This may seem rather juvenile. I do it any time I'm drinking with friends. Doctor Everly showed me how. It's an exercise he taught me to improve manual dexterity. You see, as well as stumbling a lot, I'm clumsy with my hands also."

Then it was his turn to be startled. Barris mouthed an oath and, with a sweeping motion, cleared the table, knocking all three glasses to the floor, wetting the tabletop with spilled whiskey. With a fine show of injured indignation, he declared,

"I don't take kindly to such foolery, damnitall! I call it an insult!"

"Please," frowned George. "I meant no offense."

"I'm as offended as my friend," Cordeau said sternly. "When you're accepting another man's hospitality, it's hardly polite to fool with the drinks."

In vain George mumbled apologies. The killers rose and moved out of the bar, refraining from comment until they had passed through the lobby and were climbing the stairs.

"Sonofabitch," breathed the sweating Barris. "Hell, Frenchy, we never ran into *this* kind of mark before. I swear, when he started moving those glasses around . . . !"

"An exercise to improve manual dexterity," Cordeau said in disgust. "No matter, Carl."

"No matter you say?" challenged Barris. "Two tries? Two misses?"

"I'll take care of him after he retires," muttered Cordeau. "The old cushion over the face routine. Perfect for an idiot like Middleton — and I'm good at it. No signs of violence. A physician in a town as no-account as Tyson could never detect the difference between asphyxiation and heart failure."

Down below, George rose and hesitantly approached the stony-faced custodian of the bar.

"I'm extremely sorry . . . " he began.

"Uh huh," grunted the barkeep.

And his disapproving eyes flicked from George's abashed face to the scattered glass and the liquor stains on the floor.

"A small shot of rye, if you please," begged George, proffering a $10 bill. "And, please, no change. I feel I should recompense the management for the broken glasses and — uh — any inconvenience caused."

As he obliged, the barkeep grudgingly remarked,

"Wasn't you spilled the drinks."

"Well, no," agreed George. "But I feel responsible."

He downed his shot at the bar and, feeling a little steadier for it, nodded goodnight to the barkeep and removed himself to the lobby. The desk clerk was having a bad time it seemed. A large, excitable female, one of George's fellow-passengers on the north run, was demanding to be transferred to another room and, at some length, explaining her problem, the clerk hard-pressed to get a word in edgewise.

"It wasn't until I'd finished supper and went to the room that I realized the window faces east. I simply cannot sleep in a bedroom facing east. It just has to face west. Walter could tell you. Walter — that's my husband . . . "

"I'm sorry, Mrs Crombie, but . . . " began the clerk.

"Who better than Walter would understand this phobia of mine?" she challenged. "We've been separated only two days and, already, I miss him so. That dear man is so attentive — and so ardent. We've been married fifteen years and dear Walter is still *ardent.*"

"You're a lucky lady, but about the room . . . "

"When we moved into our home in Collinsburg, I had to insist the upstairs parlor, which faced west, should become our bedroom, but dear Walter never protested. He understands about my condition, you see. So the parlor furniture had to be transferred to the room opposite and the bedroom furniture transferred to the room that used to be the parlor — with the window facing west. It's just something I can't control, as I'm sure you'll understand."

"I do understand, ma'am," sighed the clerk. "But, like I told you, we're full up tonight. No vacant rooms, no way I can change you to a room on the west side unless another guest agrees to switch with you."

"Excuse me," said George, drawing closer. "Forgive the intrusion, but I couldn't help overhearing . . . "

"You're Mister Middleton," announced the big woman. "The nice young man from the stagecoach."

"The same," he nodded. "And . . . "

"Bound for Lamont, Nebraska, to attend a wedding I believe you said," she smiled. "How very pleasant for you, Mister Middleton. My destination is Keilby. That's about thirty miles north of Lamont. My sister Lavinia is recuperating from an illness and I just *have* to visit her. Walter must be missing me so, but I had to insist on traveling alone. He has to mind the store, you see. We have a general store in Collinsburg — nothing but good quality merchandise stocked. I need my sleep and I can't *possibly* sleep in a bedroom facing east and, if I'm awake all night, I'll be exhausted by the time I reach Keilby and my dear sister. She's recuperating from . . . " She broke off to frown at the mumbling, exasperated clerk. "Did you say something?"

"No, ma'am, I didn't," said the clerk. "But I think this gentleman was about to say something." He eyed George in desperation. "Right, mister?"

"I'm in Room Nine," offered George, "and I was about to ask . . . "

"Room Nine faces west," the clerk said eagerly. "Mrs Crumb . . . "

"Crombie," corrected the big woman.

"Pardon, Mrs Crombie." The clerk was gamely tight-reining his impatience. "That's right, mister. Your room faces west and the lady's directly opposite. So, if you . . . ?"

"I'd be only to pleased, Mrs Crombie," said George. "It will take me but a moment to repack my grip and make the change."

"I hadn't begun to unpack!" she exclaimed. "Oh, this is so obliging of you! Could we change our things over right away?"

"Right away," he smiled, taking her arm, conducting her to the stairs.

"You're much younger than my Walter — well, naturally," she cooed, as they climbed the stairs. "But you do remind me of him because he too is a perfect gentleman, always so considerate. And ardent, very ardent."

Within a few minutes, gentle George and the full-figured Harriet Crombie had changed rooms and traded keys and were settling down for the night.

It was 1.15 a.m. and the settlement of Tyson was closed down and tomb-quiet when Cordeau quit the room he shared with his partner by way of the window and crept along the second floor gallery to the open window of Room 9.

Stealthily he climbed in. His bootless feet made no sound as he took two paces forward and scanned the room. The bed and its slumbering occupant were in darkness. The only illumination was the moonlight shafting through the window, offering him a clear view of a chair, its seat adorned by a loose cushion. He reached for the cushion and crept to the bed, holding it in front of him, ready to press it to the sleeper's face, to press down hard, pinning his victim, making breathing impossible.

In the act of covering the dimly visible face, he tensed. His scalp crawled as the sleeper came alive. He was shocked to hear a female voice, to feel her eager hands grabbing at him.

"Walter — darling Walter — you impulsive, ardent man you! Come to me, Walter . . . !"

There was only one thing Cordeau

could do, and he did it fast. He sprang clear of the bed, flung the cushion away and made a beeline for the window, diving through head-first, then scurrying away.

For a while, Harriet Crombie, wife of ardent Walter, was in a state of confusion, wondering if she'd been dreaming. She heaved herself to a sitting posture, felt at the bedside table, found matches, scratched one to life and raised the funnel of the lamp. She touched the match to the wick, lowered the funnel and, by the light of the lamp, gazed about dazedly. She knuckled at her eyes, meditated a long moment, then extinguished the lamp and lowered her head to the pillow.

'It *had* to be a dream,' she decided, just before sleep reclaimed her. 'Ah, Walter, my ardent one. I'm so concerned for dear Lavinia — but you are ever in my thoughts . . . '

* * *

At 7.45 a.m., while toting their valises to the stage depot, the killers traded comments.

"I still don't understand it," grouched Barris. "An old pro like Frenchy Cordeau — climbing into the wrong room."

"I don't want to hear you say that again", scowled Cordeau. "It was the *right* room, but Middleton wasn't sleeping there."

"He switched rooms?"

"Only explanation."

"Well, damnitall, we got a fee to earn."

"There's still time — ample time. I have a better idea now. We're going on to Lamont. Haven't I always said the bigger the crowd the easier we score? That's where we're gonna eliminate Middleton — at that wedding banquet — with a lot of citizens milling around."

"Knife at close quarters, huh?"

"Best way. By the time he falls, by the time the screaming starts, I'll be well and truly clear of him. Nothing to it, Carl. Remember the Dodge City job?"

"Big crowd. Fourth of July parade, the sidewalks packed. Yeah. You handled that one mighty smooth."

"Believe me, we'll finish him in Lamont."

"I guess everything's going our way. There were just two seats vacant on this coach," said Barris.

The other north-bound passengers were waiting to board the stage, watching the guard secure their baggage on the roof. Cordeau and Barris surrendered their valises and appraised their fellow-travelers, Cordeau nodding curtly in response to George's hesitant greeting. The Dakota-bound cattle-buyer wore a distinctly hungover look. They pegged the sallow-complexioned character in tan derby and checkered suit to be a drummer. Big Harriet Crombie was not immediately recognized by Cordeau. Obeying the driver's command, they climbed aboard. A moment later the stage was rolling out of town and the passengers getting settled, throwing out a few conversational openers.

The big woman led off by announcing she had experienced something quite startling in the wee small hours, part dream, part reality — or maybe she had imagined some of it. Cordeau eyed her warily. George showed polite interest. The cattle-buyer grunted, slumped low in his seat and tipped his hat over his eyes. The man in the checkered suit raised an eyebrow. For Harriet Crombie, this was encouragement enough. She launched into a melodramatic description of the incident and, upon learning of the room switch, Cordeau and Barris became impassive.

At the end of her rambling dissertation, George waxed solicitous.

"I'm sure we're all sorry, Mrs Crombie, very sorry for the alarm and confusion you must have suffered."

"I can't really say I was alarmed," she frowned. "I was so sure, you see, that Walter had joined me." She amended that. "*If* there was a man in my room. If I didn't imagine it all."

The killers stayed impassive when the man in the checkered suit spoke up, though his mention of his profession came as a shock.

"You'd have been welcome to my help, ma'am, if you'd been really frightened," he assured her. "Raymond's the name, Vint Raymond. I introduced myself yesterday, but didn't feel any need to explain I'm a Deputy U.S. marshal." He delved into a pocket for his badge. "Haven't been wearing this. I won't be on official duty again till I leave the coach at Grey Rock, up by the Dakota border. On my way there to testify at a murder trial."

"I must say I'd have felt safer," beamed Mrs Crombie, "knowing a Federal officer was sleeping only a few doors away."

"You checked your belongings, I take it?" asked Raymond.

"Oh, yes," she nodded.

"And nothing is missing?" frowned George.

"Nothing at all," she assured him.

"Could still have been a robbery attempt," opined Raymond. "The thief didn't count on your coming awake."

"Good heavens!" she gasped.

"Stay calm, ma'am," he soothed. "My guess is you gave him a bad scare waking up that way, grabbing at him. Plain enough he's not one of the violent kind. So you were never really in danger."

"Best put it out of your mind, ma'am," advised Cordeau.

"It's over and done with," nodded Barris.

"You gents traveling far?" Raymond casually enquired.

"Might try our luck in Lamont or some other big town," offered Cordeau.

"Sporting men," said Raymond, nodding knowingly.

"We do bar work too," said Cordeau.

"Wait on tables," said Barris.

"In better class restaurants of course,"

drawled Cordeau. "Always an honest dollar to be turned by a couple of willing hands, right Marshal?"

"Why, sure," agreed Raymond. "And you'll probably find work at Lamont. If what I hear is true, that's a mighty fast-growing town."

Conversation lapsed for a mile or so. George then remarked to the Federal man.

"I too am to be a witness at a murder trial. In my hometown, that is. Shadlow, Kansas?"

"That so?" Raymond showed only mild interest. "Prosecution or defense?"

"Prosecution," said George. "As a matter of fact, I'll be the county's only witness."

"Quite a responsibility," shrugged Raymond. "But you seem like a steady young feller. I guess you can handle it."

* * *

The Joels of St Louis had begun their journey on schedule, had connected with a westbound in Omaha and, on the morning the northbound stage left Tyson, were sharing a Pullman car with some 14 other travelers. Already, Stella was missing the privacy of the compartment reserved for the family on the northwest stage of their journey. Her genial husband mollified her with his assurance they would reach their destination mid-morning of the morrow.

"We stay overnight in Dawson Ford, leave quite early tomorrow morning and, according to the conductor . . . "

"A dour individual," she sniffed. "I think Claudette is quite terrified of him."

"Surely not," he protested. "I found him to be a courteous fellow."

"And probably kind to his wife and children," sighed Stella. "But then Claudette is terrified of everyone."

They had two double seats to themselves at this time. Seated opposite them, the demurely gowned and bonneted Claudette fidgeted with a handkerchief and made a valiant effort to smile.

"I'm enjoying the trip," she assured them. "Honestly."

"Of course, and why shouldn't you?" nodded Lester, smiling encouragingly. "The other passengers are quite respectable. You agree, my dear? It could have been so much worse. No riff-raff aboard."

Stella dropped her voice.

"The person seated across the passage from us is, I believe, a traveling salesman."

"We must expect to encounter a drummer or two," he shrugged. "And you know, they aren't all flashy, flamboyant types with loud voices. The one you speak of, for instance, seems a gentle soul and quite presentable."

The salesman, soberly garbed and keeping pretty much to himself, did not address the Joels until the westbound rolled to a halt at a water stop on the route west. Claudette glanced out the window and at once expressed alarm. There were red-skins here, grouped by the platform supporting the tank, some of them in conversation with the railroad employee manning this lonely post.

"Indians!" she gasped.

Moving along the aisle, the conductor droned,

"Quarter-hour stop, folks. Anybody wanting to stretch his legs, here's your chance. We take on water here."

He moved on, apparently oblivious to Claudette's agitation and her mother's efforts to calm her. It was then that the elderly drummer doffed his derby, identified himself and, fixing a fatherly grin on Claudette, told her,

"We've nothing to fear from these Indians. They're of the Otoe tribe and peaceable. I travel this route all the time, Miss . . . "

"The name, is Joel, Mister Beck," offered Lester.

"Mister and Mrs Joel, Miss Joel, my pleasure," Orin Beck said affably. "As I was saying, Miss Joel, I've met these Otoes often. Been many a long year since they were warlike. Nowadays, they just run up rugs and string beads and fashion trinkets to sell to the tourists. That's why they're out there now. Notice how the tank attendant's socializing with them? He's Morty Burrows, old identity in these parts. Even speaks the Otoe dialect."

"They're quite harmless, Mister Beck?" frowned Stella.

"Take my word for it," nodded Beck.

"Then let's stretch our legs by all means," smiled Lester. "Might as well take the fresh air, Stella my dear. Come, Claudette, join us."

Of the passengers descending from the Pullmans to ease their cramped limbs, one aroused the immediate interest of the eldest Otoe here present. Once a mighty hunter, this veteran considered himself the super-salesman of his tribe, the wiliest psychologist and the smartest pitch-man. Claudette's self-consciousness was manifest; he didn't need to be much of a psychologist to peg her as an easy mark. She cringed as he confronted her, proffering a thin strap of rawhide, knotted and with a battered medallion dangling from it. He mumbled solemnly, earnestly, incomprehensibly.

"Really, Lester . . . " began Stella.

"Don't distress yourself," he chided. "And Claudette, my dear, don't be afraid. The poor old fellow isn't threatening you."

Overhearing this, the scrawny, overalled Morty Burrows moved across to howdy these city folks and ease Claudette's fears.

"Old Pashanto wouldn't want to faze the little lady. Why, I've known him for years."

"I'm told you understand the language," prodded Lester. "Perhaps you'd be kind enough to translate?"

"To do what, Mister?"

"My daughter's alarm will be eased, I'm sure, if you could tell us what the old man is saying to her."

"Oh, sure," shrugged Burrows. "Glad

to oblige." He mumbled at old Pashanto in the Otoe dialect. Pashanto mumbled back at him — at some length. "Uh huh, yeah. That a fact? Well, all right then."

"What exactly?" demanded Lester.

For him, Morty Burrows' translation was almost as incomprehensible as the original, but he persisted until Pashanto's claims were made clearer. The medallion, it seemed, bore a likeness of a wolf's head and commemorated the Otoe tribe's most honored ancestor, Chief Wolf Tooth, legendary warrior famed for his great courage. It was, or so Pashanto insisted, a charm and strong medicine. Those who wore the medallion acquired courage when they most needed it and would never be laking in confidence.

"She'll just never be spooked again, Pashanto claims," Burrows declared in conclusion.

"Spooked?" frowned Stella.

"Well," shrugged Burrows. "Meanin' there ain't nothin' can scare her while she's wearin' this trinket."

"Ridiculous," sniffed Stella.

"I want to have it," Claudette said quickly. "Please, Papa, may I?"

"Oh, come now, child . . . " began Stella.

"Where's the harm? Lester challenged with a good-humored grin. "The price?"

"Pashanto says a couple dollars," drawled Burrows.

"Little to pay for something she so desires, Stella," remarked Lester, parting with the money.

Pashanto hung the bauble carefully avoiding contact with the flowered bonnet. It hung on her bosom. Noting this, and wincing, Stella promptly ordered,

"Tuck it inside."

Claudette obeyed, smiling happily and announced,

"I think I'll go back to the carriage now. Thank you, Papa."

Some ten minutes later, watching the westbound steam away, Burrows slanted a sly grin at his old crony.

"Easy Wampum, huh Chief?"

In the Pullman car, to the astonishment of her parents, Claudette moved across the aisle, took the seat opposite the drummer's and began engaging him in conversation. He folded and discarded his newspaper and responded like a fond uncle. The conductor came trudging by and was accorded a cheery greeting.

"We're having a comfortable journey," Claudette informed him with a bright smile. "This is really a fine train."

The dour conductor's visage creased in a genial grin.

"The railroad appreciates you saying it, Miss. We try to please."

He touched his cap and moved on, while the Joels traded bemused stares.

"I don't believe this is happening!" breathed Stella. "And I certainly don't believe in charms or magical spells or any such fiddle-faddle!"

"Nor do I, my dear," Lester said softly. "But I believe I understand what is happening to our beloved Claudette."

6

The Un-Co-operative Target

A MILE from the water-stop, an alien sound was carried to Stella Joel's busy ears. The voice was undoubtedly her daughter's, but the sound uncharacteristic.

"She's *laughing*!" she whispered to her husband.

"She finds Mister Beck amusing and congenial company," guessed Lester. "Personally I'm delighted she's so happy. I get the impression he's entertaining her with anecdotes of his travels. Where's the harm?"

"If you can explain this incredible situation, please do so," she begged. "Lester, it's quite beyond me!"

"It's not the Indian charm," he said. "It's the girl's *belief* in the thing. Obviously, while ever she believes the old redskin's claim, she'll draw courage from it. We needn't concern ourselves, my dear. A lot of people are superstitious, some of them quite intelligent and well known to us. Take Leon Baume for instance . . . "

"The banker?"

"One of our regular patrons. I have it on good authority he's positively terrified of the number thirteen. And Chester Rodney, president of the De Soto Shipping Line? Inveterate gambler, Mister Rodney. At the Bon Chance Casino there is only one chair he will use. That, he insists, is his lucky chair. He truly believes that, just as Claudette believes the medallion can cure her shyness."

"She believes because she *wants* to believe?" frowned Stella. "Heavens, Lester, that's self-hypnosis."

"What matter?" he smiled. "For years we've hoped and prayed our daughter would come out of her shell, and now it's happening. No cause for dismay, Stella. Let's be grateful — and enjoy it while it lasts."

"Perhaps," Stella said hopefully, "this wedding won't be the ordeal I anticipated."

Claudette's new confidence was still manifest when, 10.15 of the following morning, the westbound reached the Lamont depot and the Joels and Dodds of Lamont came forward to offer the family a warm welcome. The brothers shook hands, the sisters-in-law kissed and the bride-to-be was hugged by all. Well to the fore was the bow-legged, effusive Yancey, eager to present his good-humored, still comely wife to the visitors. Mayor Lingard was on hand, his amiable smile a fixture. And to ensure a favorable impression of local law enforcement, Big Bart Whitney put in an appearance, long hair, fancy vest, ivory-butted Colts and all. Max Joel, who had inherited his father's courtly manners, presented himself to his cousin Claudette and offered his compliments, backed by his smiling brother, while Stella watched her daughter anxiously and wondered if she would shrink from them. She need not have worried. The new, sedate Miss Joel conversed easily with her cousins and the future Mrs Max Joel and, for a few moments, linked arms with the father of the bride-to-be, who looked her over and gleefully remarked.

"By dawg! Gonna be many a purty filly at this hitchin', but I swear Miss Claudette's gonna shine!" He doffed his hat and kissed Claudette's cheek. "Keep smilin', honey, and all them buck bachelors gonna be fightin' over you."

"Really, Mister Dodd, you'll be turning her head," protested Stella.

The new arrivals were conducted bag and baggage to the vehicles that would take them to J Bar, the Dodds having explained they would now wait for the Chadwicks, due on the 2 p.m. train from Denver.

To the Savoy Yancey and his womenfolk retreated, there to relax as the mayor's guests, have lunch and be on hand to meet the eastbound. It was then, while Lingard was conducting the Dodds up the steps to the hotel's imposing entrance, that the tall strangers caught their first glimpse of the fair Mary Sue.

The Texans were emerging from the premises of tailor Barney Glennis at this time. Glennis, dapper and congenial, had measured them for their wedding suits and promised delivery in ample time for the great day. Now, following their glance, he identified Lingard's guests for them.

"She'll be a sight to see when old Yancey walks her down that centre aisle," he declared. "And the groom won't let her down, believe me. Mighty handsome young feller, Max Joel."

"Sure is a looker, huh runt?" enthused Stretch.

"Purty as paint," observed Larry. "It's startin' to feel like a joyful function already, this weddin'."

"Listen — uh — you sure you won't

change your minds?" asked the tailor. "For the pants of these fine black suits, beltloops just aren't right. They hang better, look better, if you wear suspenders."

"Belts," Larry said firmly.

"Oh, well . . . " shrugged Glennis.

The eastbound was as punctual as the train that had brought the St Louis Joels to Lamont. Again, the mayor and the celebrated scourge of the lawless were on hand, joining the Dodds on the platform for the welcome ceremony. Again a surrey and wagon waited in readiness to transport guests and baggage, these vehicles to be escorted by the Block D foreman and a half-dozen riders. Myra and daughter embraced Jerome and the gracious Hildegard, the bride-to-be was admired by all and rough-hewn Yancey guarded his tongue and looked to his manners.

Archer Hallam, having witnessed the reception, quit the depot and strolled along Main to the Clayton Casino, his gaze on the moving Block D rigs and their occupants, also the seven-rider escort. A few moments later he was reporting to the casino's proprietor.

"So they've arrived," grinned Clayton. "And now we only need wait for the wedding day."

"I guess we'll get our best chance at the Savoy," frowned Hallam, "while they're drinking and dancing."

"Got any better ideas, Arch?" challenged Clayton. "Like to try breaking into Dodds ranch-house, searching the Chadwick woman's bedroom while she's asleep — even if you could find your way to it in a house as big as old Yancey's? First you'd have to get past the servant's quarters and the bunkhouse gang. Then you'd have to . . ."

"All right," nodded Hallam. "You made your point."

At sundown of that day, when the northbound stage reached the Lamont depot, George Middleton was first to alight. He made a small ceremony of assisting Mrs Crombie from the vehicle, collected his grip and entered the office to question the tired-eyed, very bored ticket clerk.

"No," said the clerk. "Haven't seen any Block D hands in town, not since the folks from Denver arrived."

"I expected to be met," explained George. He made to prop an elbow on the counter, missed and slumped, coming dangerously close to injuring his jaw. Straightening up while the clerk surveyed him warily, he announced, "I'm here for the wedding."

"One of the guests, huh?" prodded the clerk.

"A cousin of Mrs Yancey Dodd," said George.

"That's nice," remarked the clerk, his tone suggesting indifference. "Ought to be a right fine wedding."

"Well," sighed George, picking up his grip. "If Cousin Myra hasn't sent a rig to take me to Block D . . . "

"They know you were coming in on this stage?" asked the clerk.

"Well, naturally I mailed off my acceptance of the invitation," frowned George. Then he winced in embarrassment. "But it now occurs to me — I didn't think to wire them my time of arrival."

"Uh huh," grunted the clerk.

George departed in disorder. It was a typical Middleton exit; he tripped while emerging from the doorway, but managed to regain his balance, which was at least preferable to going down flat on his face.

Cordeau and Barris had chosen to leave their bags on the depot porch for the time being. They were watching from the opposite sidewalk when their intended victim moved off, toting his grip, ready to ask directions to Block D.

"We'll tag him a while," Cordeau decided. "It's getting dark."

"We might get a break," nodded Barris. "And, personally, I've had my bellyful of that jackass, like to get this job over and done with."

It was one of those coincidences that do happen. George was loath to accost any of the five Lamont men he passed while trudging uptown. To his nervous eye, these fairly harmless citizens seemed unkempt and forbidding, certainly not the kind to oblige a stranger. The young woman crossing the street, arms laden with parcels, seemed more the kind he could confidently approach. He admired her demeanor, her graceful movements. Obviously a lady, he decided, as he quickened his step.

Lounging in canebacks near the street-door to the *Pioneer* office, the Texans watched Abby moving toward them. They yawned and shifted in their seats, making ready to rise and relive her of her burden. From the mouth of the next alley south, the lynx-eyed professionals decided another opportunity was presenting itself; George too was crossing the street, hurrying to intercept the young woman.

"His back'll be turned my way,"

muttered Cordeau, easing a tool of his trade from the sheath concealed by his coat-sleeve, "And the timing's right."

George reached the sidewalk close behind Abby, turned to confront her and, with a flourish, doffed his derby.

"Good evening, madam. Would you be so kind — oops . . . !"

"Drat!" said Abby.

Ninety-nine men out of a hundred could have accorded her the courtesy of bearing their heads without bumping her elbow and causing her to drop her parcels, but, of course, George was Number 100. He gasped an apology and bent to retrieve the fallen articles. She bent at that same time with the inevitable result; they bumped heads.

"Ouch!"

"I'm most desperately sorry — I do apologize . . . "

It was the thudding sound, not loud, but close at hand, that distracted the Texans' amused gaze from Abby and George. For exactly one-and-a-half seconds they were staring at the knife embedded in a post supporting the awning, watching its hilt quivering, then they were out of their chairs, Larry to move to the knife, Stretch to whirl and dash for the nearest alley south.

Unaware of George's close call, as oblivious as George himself, Abby was on her knees now and suggesting,

"It might be safer — for both of us — if you just stand clear. No offense, but you're disaster on two feet."

"That's been said before, I regret to say," he sighed. "But you must allow me to help — if I promise to be careful!"

After tugging the knife from the post, slipping it into his belt and subjecting the clumsy stranger to a brief once-over, Larry took to his heels. He caught up with his cursing sidekick in the alley paralleling Main on the west side.

"Didn't even spot the sonofabitch," Stretch complained. "But where else could he have throwed it from? Had to be the side alley. If he'd made his getaway along the street, we'd have sighted him for sure. So he had to get lost around here someplace."

They glanced to left and right. The alley was long, running level with the main stem for better than three blocks. And no fleeing figure in view.

"Too many hideaway holes," Larry said in disgust. "Too many places he could get lost before you got to where we are."

"It irks me, and then some," scowled Stretch. "Some bastard tried for the tanglefoot and . . . "

"Tanglefoot would've taken this in his back — right before our eyes — if he wasn't so blame clumsy," declared Larry. They retreated into the side alley to the light shafting out of a window. He drew the knife from his belt. Stretch bent to study it as he hefted it, testing its balance. "Quite a time since we saw one of these, huh?"

"Throwin' knife, yup," grunted Stretch. "That's what it is sure enough."

"Made especially for puttin' in a target, but not from close quarters," nodded Larry, returning it to his belt. "And that takes skill, beanpole."

"Ain't that the truth," agreed Stretch. "He had to be a real pro, him that threw it." A disquieting thought occurred to him. "Hey — uh — I guess he was aimin' at the young feller — not Abby?"

"When the young feller bent and batted heads with Abby, the knife hit the post blade-first," growled Larry. "*He* was the target, bet your double-cinched saddle on that."

"We gonna tell ol' Big Butt?" asked Stretch.

"Maybe, but not rightaway," said Larry. "I'm some curious about the young feller, like to learn a thing or two about . . . "

"So here we go again," Stretch said resignedly.

"Meanin'?" asked Larry.

"You know what I mean," said Stretch. "I heard you say it out of your own mouth, runt. You're curious again. We're supposed to be bodyguardin'

Milo, but now some dumb stranger near takes a knife in his back and you got to play detective."

"Let's get back to him," urged Larry.

In desperate need to get out of sight fast, the killers had sidled through a brightly-lit rear doorway. Their tension at once eased. They were in a kitchen, the largest, best-appointed, busiest kitchen they had seen since their last visit to Denver. Cordeau counted no fewer than four kitchen-hands and glimpsed three white-jacketed waiters carrying laden trays through the swing doors to his left. The cooking range extended almost a wall-length. Plainly, the party in charge here, the double-chinned chef, resented this intrusion. He made that clear by confronting them and informing them his domain was off limits to guests of the Savoy Hotel.

Cordeau, first to rally, addressed the chef respectfully.

"Corbin's the name, sir. May I present my friend Barker? We aren't guests. It just happens we're looking for work, and hotel work is our specialty.

Taking his cue, Barris explained,

"We've had plenty experience in the hotel business, every chore you could name. We've been porters, kitchen-hands . . . "

"Working all the better hotels, you understand," said Cordeau. "And one glance at your kitchen indicates this must be the finest hotel in Lamont."

"You won't find better in the state capital or even Kansas City," frowned the chef. "So you're particular where you work your trade, huh?"

"And we give satisfaction," Cordeau assured him. "Bar work would suit us, sir. We've had a great many years' experience as bartenders, stewards . . . "

"No extra help needed right now," said the chef. "You probably heard about the big wedding reception here?"

"Well, yes, and I thought . . . " began Cordeau.

"Sure," nodded the chef. "But the boss, Mayor Lingard, keeps the place well-staffed. We have all the hands we'll need when the big day arrives, won't need to put on any extra men."

"Naturally we're disappointed," said Cordeau. "But keep us in mind? We'll probably stay a week or two. If your boss changes his mind, we'll be available."

"Yeah, sure," said the chef. "I'll remember you. Corbin and . . . ?"

"Barker." said Barris.

"We won't be hard to find," drawled Cordeau. "Passed a smaller place on our way uptown, come to think of it. The Kermond House? We'll probably check in there."

"So I'll know where to find you," the chef said impatiently. "That's all, boys. We're busy this time of evening, so . . . "

"We know how it is," said Cordeau, retreating to the rear door.

"Nice talking to you," Barris said politely.

Cordeau was cold calm when they made for the stage depot to collect their baggage, but Barris was jumpy. From the depot, they toted their bags toward the Kermond House, Cordeau muttering reprimands.

"Take it easy. So we missed again? No matter. There's still the wedding celebration."

"I'm getting a bad feeling about this one," complained Barris. "What's the matter with us? We jinxed all of a sudden? Four tries, Frenchy. Four misses. Not our usual style — not so you'd notice."

"Freak luck," shrugged Cordeau. "Coincidence. We'll rent a room, find a cafe where the food's to our expensive taste and decide our next move."

Returning to the newspaper office, the Texans found the young stranger in conversation with Abby and her father. Milo had wheeled himself to the street doorway to investigate the commotion. Having taken her parcels into the office. Abby was now sizing up the new arrival. She was only casually interested, just being polite.

More than casually interested Larry studied the inept newcomer and lent an attentive ear.

Milo was ready with a solution to Mr George Middleton's small problem, that problem being how to get to Block D.

"You're in luck, young feller," he offered, his gaze switching to the surrey slowly approaching along Main Street. "I happen to know my friend Doc Parrish is headed out to Dodd spread right now. He'll oblige you, I'm sure."

"I'd be most grateful," said George. "And, Miss Fenner, I apologize again for my clumsiness."

"One apology is ample," shrugged Abby. "That makes your fifth. I've been keeping count." She turned to her father. "How on earth do you keep track of people's movements, stuck in the office in your wheelchair?"

"No trick to it," said Milo. "Doc looked in on me a little while ago, mentioned he'd been sent for. Seems a Block D man took a fall this afternoon, suffered some kind of head injury."

"Something else I'm curious about," Abby told the tall men, after introducing them to George. "You made yourselves scarce, and very quickly, right after our little accident. What was that all about?"

Larry's face became blank. Stretch looked away. So Abby and young George were none the wiser, unaware of his close call? So much the better, Larry decided. Doc Parrish was turning his matched bays toward the Pioneer building in response to Milo's beckoning. Maybe an explanation was called for. On the other hand, maybe this wasn't the time for it.

"We had to see a man about somethin'," he said nonchalantly.

"Listen, I feel like ridin' and my cayuse could use some exercise." He nodded affably to George. "Guess I'll travel along with you, kind of keep an eye on you and Doc 'case you run into proddy cowhands, the kind who play rough."

"You really think that's necessary?" frowned Abby.

"Takes only one of us to sit guard on Milo," he remarked. "Stretch'll be hangin' around."

Parrish stalled his rig, listened to Milo's request and accorded George a doleful nod.

"I'm much obliged, Doctor," said George.

Milo and daughter traded frowns, but the Texans showed no reaction to George's awkward action. He managed the simple chore of stashing his bag on the back seat, but climbing in to join the driver was something else. His foot slipped. He slumped with his head and shoulders on Parrish's lap and his legs dangling. With help from the medico, he achieved a safe sitting posture, adjusted the tilt of his derby and took a firm grip of the seat-arm.

"Sorry." He shrugged apologetically. "I *am* a shade awkward, I regret to say."

"We noticed," Parrish said woodenly.

"Won't take me long to saddle up," said Larry, turning away. "I'll be keeping you company far as Block D, Doc. Whichaway from here?"

"Northeast fork," said Parrish. "About fifty yards north of town."

Some little time later, when Larry overtook them and nudged the sorrel level with the front seat, George was making an effort to draw the lugubrious healer into conversation, telling of his eagerness to be reunited with well-loved relatives, his fondness for weddings, family get-togethers and any other kind of social function. Parrish boredly drawled a rejoinder; he conceded weddings were a matter of necessity.

"As necessary as funerals," was how he put it. "But the festivities that follow, the feverish overeating, the endless toasts and speeches are nothing but trouble for a cattle town physician. Day after the celebration, eighty per cent of the male guests are in and out of my surgery from sunrise to noon. Hangovers. Digestion troubles. Bad liver conditions and the like."

"I don't anticipate troubling you the day after the wedding, Doctor," George assured him. "I'm not teetotal, but I never over-indulge." He glanced Larry's way. "Most friendly of you, sir, to appoint yourself my escort."

"Think nothin' of it, young George," drawled Larry. "And nobody calls me sir."

"Mister Valentine then," smiled George.

"Larry to my friends," insisted Larry. "You travel far for this weddin'?"

"From Shadlow, Kansas," offered George. "I work at the bank there. Junior cashier. Most fortunate I was due for a vacation when Cousin Myra's invitation arrived."

"I'd guess the bankin' business is just right for a gent like you," remarked Larry. "Got plenty friends in the old hometown, huh?"

"Oh, yes," nodded George. "I enjoy a cordial relationship with the bank staff and my fellow-citizens."

"That's the life, huh Doc?" mused Larry. "Plenty friends. No enemies."

"Enemies? *Me*?" George's eyebrows shot up, "Well, I'm hardly the kind who'd make enemies."

"My patients are my enemies," Parrish said moodily. "That's how I think of 'em. After my first year in practice, fresh out of medical school, I was fearing the worst. There'd never be time for the things I enjoy doing, fishing, loafing, fiddling. I'm no brilliant musician, but my violin provides welcome therapy — whenever I have time for it — which isn't often. Well, I was right. My worst fears were confirmed. I'll be forever at the beck and call of people too foolish to stay healthy."

"George is a lucky feller," observed Larry. "Everybody likes you, huh George? Ain't nobody nowhere with a grudge? Some mean hombre who'd like to see you dead?"

"Of course not, Larry!" frowned

George. "What a question!"

"Feeling jealous, Larry," Prodded Parrish. "Get a little wistful sometimes, do you? I mean meeting up with a young gent like George, and him so popular in his home-town?"

"Enemies," shrugged Larry. "Who needs 'em?"

"And you've had more than your share," said Parrish. "Or shouldn't I say that?"

"Feel free," invited Larry. "You're only sayin' what's true."

"Enemies?" asked George, darting a nervous glance at Larry.

"Friend Larry and his compadre lead a somewhat hectic existence," explained Parrish. "Not of their own choosing, if they're to be believed. They're quite law-abiding you know. But I guess the most law-abiding of us can make enemies. There's a homesteader over Madison Flats away, for instance, who'd dearly love to blast me with a shotgun. His wife's time had come. He was hoping for a son. I delivered her of twin girls and the damn fool blames *me*." He shook his head mournfully. "Ignorance is a helluva thing."

"I'm thankful to say, of all the people I know, there's only one man who bears me any ill will," said George. "Well, I presume he resents me. But, of course, he can't harm me. He's under close guard in the Shadlow County Jail."

"You said no enemies," Larry mildly reminded him.

"If you want to call him an enemy . . . " shrugged George.

"Tried to hold up the bank," guessed Larry.

"Certainly not," protested George. "We don't have bank robberies in Shadlow. This man Keesing will be tried for murder. By coincidence, I saw him with the victim. So, naturally, I'll be testifying at the trial."

"Just you?" asked Larry.

"Just me," said George. "He denies even having been in town on the night in question, so I suppose it'll be my word against his. But enough of that.

I'm on vacation and looking forward to the wedding and seeing Cousin Myra again. The invitation was enclosed in a letter. She tells me Mary Sue, my second cousin, is now a beautiful young lady . . . "

"Oh, sure," grunted Parrish. "The bride'll be radiant, the bridegroom handsome, the women blubbering and their menfolk pickling their innards with booze and — the hell with it — a wedding's just extra work for me."

"Spotted your kinfolks in town," offered Larry. "Your Cousin Myra told it true. Miss Mary Sue is some looker."

"I'm considerably younger than my cousin," remarked George. "Come to think of it, she's considerably younger than Yancey, her husband . . . "

"And the father of the bride," interjected Parrish. "If you want to get along with Yancey, don't be forgetting that. He's very proud of it, so you'd better humor him."

Larry made no attempt to steer

the conversation back to the young cashier's involvement in an impending murder trail. He had this theory now and, being a hunch-player from way back, he would stick to it. In his over-simplified philosophy, there had to be a reason for everything. Undoubtedly an attempt had been made on gentle George's life this evening. A local could be responsible. The accused Keesing could be well connected with friends in Lamont who owed him a large favor, or maybe hoped to be handsomely rewarded for depriving the Shadlow County authorities of their star witness. It seemed just as likely George had been followed from Shadlow, which meant the knife-thrower was a new man in town. Unfortunately Lamont was seeing quite a few newcomers at this time; all roads led to Lamont and the biggest wedding in this territory's history.

When they came in sight of the rambling, brightly-lit Block D headquarters, the sprawling two-storey ranchhouse, the work corrals, bigger than average bunkhouse and other buildings, it occured to Larry the young guest would be well-protected here; chances of an assassination attempt at Block D seemed remote. But, when George Middleton next appeared in the county seat . . .

He stayed mounted and in the background when Parrish stalled his rig, when old Yancey and his womenfolk emerged from the house to offer their third guest a warm welcome. George collected his bag, thanked Parrish for the lift and was escorted inside by Myra and daughter to meet the Chadwicks of Denver. Parrish unearthed his black valise, nodded so-long to Larry and made his way to the bunkhouse to check on the concussed cowpoke. Then, as Larry wheeled his mount, the old man called to him.

"Hold on there a minute, Texas boy!"

Uncomfortable in his town suit, but

sprightly for his age, the veteran rancher crossed the yard and clambered to the top rail of the corral beside which Larry drew rein. He squatted up there and, as Larry made to produce his Durham-sack, fished out a couple of Havanas, offered one and clamped the other in his mouth.

"Have one of these, Valentine."

"Obliged," shrugged Larry.

He supplied a match, lit Yancey's cigar, then his own.

"Didn't guess I recognized you, I bet," grinned Yancey. "Didn't even guess I spotted you."

"Darned if I did," Larry admitted.

"In town," said Yancey. "You and Emerson — comin' out of the tailor shop."

"Looked you over, you and the ladies," nodded Larry. "But I'd have sworn you didn't even look our way."

"I don't miss much, trouble-shooter," chuckled Yancey. "These old peepers're are sharp as they ever was. And I don't forget nothin' neither. Like, for instance, all the newspaper stories, all the pitchers I've seen. You and Emerson. The Texas Hellers. By dawg, you're a sight for sore eyes. Listen, how'd you like invites to the weddin'?"

7

The Replacements

LARRY hooked a leg about his saddlehorn, savored the aroma of a fine Havana and showed Yancey Dodd a wry grin.

"We already got invites," he declared.

"So you're gonna be at the doin's?" Yancey asked eagerly.

"Friend of ours, one of Mary Sue's bridesmaids, wanted us along," said Larry. "Abby Fenner?"

"Oh, sure," grinned Yancey. "Hey, that's just great. You and your buddy're just what this shindig's gonna need."

"How so?" frowned Larry.

"With you two along, there's just bound to be a fight," Yancey gleefully predicated. "And ain't that what a good weddin' needs? Myra don't hold with it, her and her lawyer brother and his high-falutin' wife, but you and me know better, right? What's a weddin' without some kind of ruckus?"

"Shame on you," chided Larry.

"Shame nothin'," snorted Yancey. "I just want for the young'uns to have a real send-off."

"Mister Dodd . . . " began Larry.

"Yancey," growled Yancey.

"Fine, Yancey, call me Larry. Now, Yancey, somethin' you better savvy here and now. The beanpole and me don't plan on startin' no fight."

"Hogwash!"

"Stone-cold truth. We even got measured up for weddin' clothes. Aim to act respectable, gonna mind our manners too."

"Must be some way we can talk turkey on this. Listen, every mothers' son'll be there, so there'd have to be *some* jaspers you don't admire. You'll do it to make an old man happy, huh? Get a good fight goin', start swingin' them famous fists?"

"No chance. Hell, Yancey, we don't

hanker to tangle with Big Bart Whitney.

"We'll get *him* into the fight too!"

"Forget it, Yancey."

Yancey's mouth drooped at the corners; to him this was obviously a shattering setback. He frowned at Larry a moment, then produced a well-filled wallet.

"Make it worth your trouble," he offered. "How does five hundred apiece sound? What d'you say?"

"Now you're hurtin' my feelin's," Larry reproached him.

"Well, how about I hire you as bodyguards?" Yancey was suddenly inspired.

"Keep your money," said Larry. "Anybody needed help, we'd help 'em for free. Who needs bodyguards anyway?"

"Brother-in-law Jerry's good-lookin' wife," declared Yancey. "One of them Joel women too, the lady from Saint Louis."

"Aw, c'mon now . . . " protested Larry.

"No, I ain't foolin'," Yancey said earnestly. "The Saint Louis lady'll be wearin' a genuine ruby necklace of some kind. And Jerry's wife, doggone it, she'll be showin' off a diamond worth a fortune. If you don't read the papers, you likely never heard of it. They call it the Kuruman. So how about that? As father of the bride and the boss-host of this shindig, I'm responsible for all the guests and their valuables, ain't that so?"

"You don't need us," said Larry. "With Big Bart there, it's for sure no fool's gonna try grabbin' the jewelry." He waxed reproachful again. "Don't believe all you read about us, old timer. We never did relish trouble. Leave us alone and we'd never swing a fist nor pull a gun."

"Well, if you say so," shrugged Yancey.

"Believe it," advised Larry.

"I ain't despairin'," said Yancey. "All the bunkhouse gangs'll be in town, my bunch and the J Bar boys. Used to be a feud 'tween us and the Joels — maybe you heard?"

"We heard," nodded Larry. "And we're glad it's finished."

"Feud's over, but I got hopes." Yancey chuckled slyly. "My guess is there'll be hands from both spreads whoopin' it up at the Brandin' Iron Saloon — which just happens to be right across the street from the Savoy Hotel. Ain't that long since we quit feudin'. Some of them hotheads'll likely get to rememberin' old scores that was never settled, know what I mean? If they get drunk enough?"

"Bloodthirsty old sonofagun, ain't you?" accused Larry.

"Man gets to be rich — successful Myra calls it," grouched Yancey. "Don't mean he should forget old times, do it? Old times — rough times — better times? You and Stretch was raised in cattle country, so you know how it ought to be when a cattleman's gal hitches up with a neighbor-cattleman's boy. It's the gold ring and the preacher sayin' the word that makes it legal."

"That's a fact," Larry said sternly.

"But it's a good fight that gets a marriage started right," insisted Yancey. "Maybe just three or four young bucks scrappin'. Is that askin' too much, for gosh sakes?"

Larry couldn't suppress his mirth. Grinning broadly, he reached over to pat the old man's shoulder.

"Got to be gettin' back to town," he declared. "Got to stay clear of an old firebrand like you. The hell of it is, Yancey, you could be a bad influence on a couple peace-lovin' pilgrims like Stretch and me."

Until the tall rider was lost from sight beyond the timber to the southwest of Block D range, the old man stared wistfully after him. Then, impatiently, he descended from the corral rail to go back to the house and resume socializing with his guests.

Upon his return, Larry confided his hunches to his partner, who waxed fatalistic.

"Always happens anyway, runt. If we

came here for a buryin' or a christenin', it wouldn't make no difference. We'd have to get mixed up into some kind of deviltry. If Clayton's skunks don't try breakin' in to bust up Milo's printin' contraption, some bastard is gonna try puttin' *another* knife in the tanglefoot from Kansas and, if that don't happen, there's these high-toned females tricked out in rich trinkets that some thief'll grab at." Stretch shook his head in exasperation. "I got to say it, ol' buddy. Seems to me old Yancey'll get his wish. After the knot's tied and the folks start celebratin', there's just bound to be some kind of hassle. And maybe a big'un."

It was late when the staff of the Savoy Hotel called it a day. And, within a half-hour of trading goodnights and going their separate ways, two employees, waiters Sidney Croft and Noah Bergin, were rendered incapable of resuming duty next day.

Taking a short cut alone an alley, Croft was overtaken by a man whose face he never saw, knocked senseless and relived of the contents of his wallet; Carl Barris also thought to break his right arm.

Equally painful was the mishap that befell the other waiter. Noah Bergin, climbing the outside stairs to his second floor' room at a downtown hotel, finished his climb but lost his footing; he was later to complain that he could have been tripped. Thrown off-balance, he fell backward, hit the steps, somersaulted and ended up in the back alley with his left leg and right collarbone broken.

Breakfasting in the main dining room of the Savoy around 8 o'clock of the following morning, Cordeau and Barris were sighted by the chef, who promptly began a search for his boss. He found the mayor supervising the hanging of bunting in the ballroom; the great day was now only 48 hours away.

After listening to the chef's suggestion, Lingard heaved a sigh of relief.

"Damned fortunate, Gus."

"Well, with Noah and Sid laid up — our two best waiters — it's our best chance."

"Talk to them rightaway, Gus. If you're satisfied they're up to our standard, you'd best make them an offer. The regular Savoy pay, plus the bonus for working the wedding reception. Ask them if they can begin at once."

The killers gave the chef a respectful hearing, expressed sympathy for the immobilized waiters and declared their willingness to join the staff immediately.

"That'll be fine," the chef said gratefully. "Finish your breakfast, then come to the kitchen."

Left alone, Cordeau and Barris traded bland grins and resumed their meal.

"Nothin' to it," remarked Cordeau. "Supply and demand. Reduce the hired help and create a demand."

"This'll be a memorable function," drawled Barris. "I mean *memorable*. The happy couple might call it a bad omen — a guest checking out on their wedding day. Another knife job, right?"

"That'll depend," said Cordeau. "I'm told there'll be a couple dozen or more ranch-hands in town. They won't be among the invited guests, but you can bet they'll hold their own celebration. Might be some six-shooters popping, Carl, a lot of noise."

"Yeah, sure," nodded Barris. "Who'd pay any mind to an extra gunshot?"

"It might even be assumed an accident," said Cordeau. "Poor George cut down by a wild slug that richocheted into the banquet hall. Very sad."

"Very sad," chuckled Barris.

* * *

In the time preceding the great day, a Saturday that dawned bright and clear, all Lamont surrendered to wedding fever. Abby Fenner gave her father and the Texans a preview of her bridesmaid gown, modeling it for their appraisal.

Larry accorded her the tribute of a grin, a wink and a low whistle. Stretch heaved a sentimental sigh and swallowed a lump in his throat. Milo too could be sentimental, after his own fashion. His reaction was,

"Where is the dribbly-nosed brat I knew so well?"

The Texans took delivery of their wedding suits, tried them on for fit and decided they would endure the coming festivities without too much discomfort.

All the hands turned out at Block D to watch the radiant bride escorted from the ranch-house to a bunting-bedecked surrey by her proud parents and other relatives. All eyes then turned to the serenely beautiful, quite majestic Hildegard, impressive in a gown that complemented her fine complexion; Block D men had never seen a bauble as eye-catching as the pendant gleaming from her cleavage. Resplendent in evening attire as befitted the occasion, Hildegard's husband accorded the bug-eyed ranch-hands a genial nod. George had brushed his best suit and combed his hair with scrupulous care. He watched his step as he followed the wedding group out, over-awed by his attractive cousin and the radiant bride and the queenly Hildegard. This day, of all days, he was doggedly determined he would not disgrace his kinfolks. He would move with style, with grace, do his damnedest to emulate his courtly Cousin Jerry from Denver.

For his part, proud Yancey had done the best he could with what he had. A barber had been summoned from town to give him the full treatment and the grey striped pants, highly-polished boots and black hammertail jacket were custom-made, by golly, and his matching accessories spotless. He climbed in back to sit between his wife and daughter. His foreman, after sternly warning the bunkhouse gang against rowdy behaviour in Lamont, climbed to the driver's seat and took the reins. The hands promptly retreated to their saddled and ready horses, all but the veteran selected to drive George and the Chadwicks in the second surrey.

It was exactly 2 p.m. when the wedding party started for the county seat, two surreys drawn by well-groomed, smart-stepping, perfectly-matched teams.

"So far, everything's going fine," enthused the bride's father.

"I should hope, Yancey dear," said Myra, trading smiles with her daughter. "Our journey to the church is only just beginning. We're still on Block D range."

Keeping pace with the moving vehicles, but at a respectful distance, the excited Block D hands stole glances at the passengers, mostly ignoring the men, mostly ogling the women. From here to the church, they would continue to keep their distance. The foreman's orders had been explicit.

"Stay clear. We don't want no animals kickin' up dust to muss the ladies' finery — specially Mary Sue."

To his spouse, Yancey mumbled,

"It don't always take a whole hour to get from the spread to the county seat."

"We aren't hurrying today," she said gently, but firmly.

"Weddin' set for three o'clock," he reminded her.

"We'll travel slowly and with dignity," declared Myra.

"And the bride will be late," chuckled Mary Sue. "That's very fashionable, Dad, the bride arriving late. Almost a tradition."

"Ought to be the men do all the weddin' arrangin'," grouched Yancey. "Leave it to the men, keep the women out of it. Be whole lot easier all round."

"I wonder if Max is feeling nervous," smiled Myra.

"Not Max," opined Mary Sue. "It's my prediction everybody else will be fussing and fretting about one thing or another, and everybody except the bride and groom."

Seated opposite the wealthy Chadwicks

in the second rig, George too allowed himself a prediction.

"It will be a very happy affair, I'm sure," he offered. "The ceremony will be beautiful and the reception will proceed smoothly."

"Reliable Cousin George," Jerome remarked with a jovial grin. "The perfect wedding guest."

"You've acquired a certain poise since last we met," observed Hildegard.

These hand-out compliments warmed George's heart. He asked eagerly,

"Does it really show? I recall I'd just finished my schooling that last time we got together. I know how awkward I used to be, but I've been trying hard, you know, trying to improve myself."

"You did stumble while boarding this vehicle," shrugged Jerome. "But why worry, George? Everybody stumbles at one time or another. You shouldn't be self-conscious about it."

"Forgive my staring Hildegard," begged George. "You can't really blame me. So that's the fabulous

Kuruman diamond?"

"Quite beautiful, isn't it?" smiled Hildegard.

"Of course a treasure of such reputation needs the right setting," drawled Jerome. "That's why I was determined to acquire it — for Hildegard."

"It could not appear so dazzling," George said gallantly, "worn by any other lady."

"Jerry, dear, he *has* improved," chuckled Hildegard.

"Clumsy of movement," George said with a rueful grin. "But I do try to *sound* suave."

With less distance to travel, the J Bar family and guests were now playing the scene enacted at Block D a quarter-hour ago. Max Joel and his brother had never appeared so handsome, so assured, to their doting mother. Amy Joel, a lady of slight physique and of similar temperament to her friend Myra Dodd, emerged from the impressive sandstone ranch-house with her husband and his relatives and, upon sighting her sons, heaved a sigh and wistfully observed,

"Just look at those boys, for heaven's sake. Not a trace of nerves!"

"Let's call that a good omen," suggested her husband. The gentleman-rancher had never looked as distinguished; his brother was secretly envying the cut of his clothes and his courtly bearing. "If Mary Sue is as composed as Max — and I'm sure she is — the ceremony will be unmarred by awkward moments. I've always felt a wedding ceremony should be conducted with dignity and polish. You agree, Stella?"

"Absolutely, Ralph," said his sister-in-law.

Stella then moved forward to link arms with Amy, thus positioning herself in view of the mounted escort of Joel riders, all of them bathed, clean-shaven, wearing their best clothes and, at this early stage, on their best behaviour. Like the Block D men, the J Bar men gaped on cue. Stella's ruby pendant would play second fiddle to the Kuruman diamond, but was eye-catching nevertheless.

True, the Joel brothers were in good spirits this afternoon, handsome in their wedding clothes and trading jocular remarks with the drivers of the gaily-decorated surreys. Glancing over his shoulder, the jaunty Elroy blew his mother a kiss and waved cheerily to his cousin. Claudette, still gratifying her parents with her new-found confidence, returned Elroy's wave and eagerly aimed a request at the father of the groom.

"Couldn't Elroy drive us, Uncle Ralph — please? I could travel up front with him and we could talk all the way to the church. Elroy is so *cheery*, keeps me laughing all the time . . . "

"We've heard you, honey," remarked Amy. "I declare, Stella, I've never known a girl to change so. You and Lester have done wonders with her."

"Have to watch the time," said Joel,

consulting his watch. "I suppose we'd better make a move now."

The women were handed into the waiting vehicles, the local Joels sharing the first surrey with their bridegroom-son, their younger son replacing the driver of the other surrey after boosting Claudette up to the seat. Lester and Stella made themselves comfortable, the J Bar foreman bawled a command and another wedding party began its journey to the Lamont Community Chapel.

This was, for Lester Joel, a pleasing and relaxing occasion. Only the painful shyness of their daughter could have wet-blanketed his enjoyment of this day, and now that shyness, that acute self-consciousness, was nought but a memory. Claudette, quite beautiful in her wedding attire, sitting up there with her dashing cousin, had obviously undergone a transformation. Lester had never hoped for such a change, and said as much, but quietly.

"She's so much happier."

"But how long can this last?" wondered Stella. "She's an intelligent girl, Lester. She was always shy, but never stupid. Surely, sooner or later, she'll come down to earth and realize that ugly medallion is but a curio, holding no magic power. And then what?"

"Let's not look a gift wolf in the mouth," he suggested.

"You mean gift horse," she corrected.

"I know what I mean," he countered. "I refer, my dear, to the design on the medallion, the emblem of the late Wolf Tooth."

"I never heard such a ridiculous story," she scoffed.

Abby Fenner was the subject of the conversation on the driver's seat.

"All you've told me of your lady-love is her name, the fact that she's very attractive and her father runs the local newspaper," Claudette complained. "Don't be secretive, Elroy. Tell me more — such as when are you going to propose?"

"Quite a girl, Abby," mused Elroy. "I know you'll like her. And you'll be meeting her soon enough. I think I mentioned she's one of Mary Sue's bridesmaids. The other will be Molly Lingard, the mayor's elder daughter, also very pretty. But, of course, Abby's the prettiest of them all."

"You're dodging my question," chided Claudette. "When will you propose? Why not at the reception, Elroy, maybe while you're dancing with her. That would be so romantic. Sweep her off her feet and . . . "

"I regret to confide Abby keeps her feet firmly planted on the ground," grinned Elroy. "She keeps rejecting me. Well, I suppose I can't blame her. My fault. The penalty for over-confidence. She thinks I'm conceited."

"I don't think you're conceited," declared Claugette. "I think you're urbane and very stylish and you have tremendous self-confidence, but . . . "

"Speaking of confidence, what happened to my retiring Cousin Claudette?"

he good-humoredly enquired.

"Oh? You noticed I've changed?" she asked.

"The change," said Elroy, "could hardly pass unnoticed."

"There's a quite simple explanation, she confided. "I'm under the influence of an Otoe warrior chief called Wolf Tooth. Concealed on my person is a medallion bearing a likeness of the animal after which he was named."

"A lucky charm?" Elroy asked uncertainly.

"While ever I wear it, I am immune to embarrassment," she assured him. "I have confidence, all the confidence I once lacked."

At that point, Elroy deemed it wise to change the subject.

"Tell me about Saint Louis," he urged.

* * *

In the banquet room of the Savoy Hotel, Eugene Lingard was addressing the assembled staff, which now included Frenchy Cordeau and Carl Barris, their white jackets spotless, camouflaging their armpit holstered Smith & Wesson .38's. The hotel-owner expressed his confidence that, for this great occasion, his employees would uphold the Savoy's highest tradition of service to distinguished guest, etc. It was a brief address of necessity; he would soon be accompanying his wife and daughters to the church.

In his surgery, long-faced Doc Parrish was preparing for the worst, carefully checking his medical cabinet.

"Let's see now. That one's slow-acting, but a sure cure for a hangover. Plenty of that on hand, fortunately. Iodine? Yes, in good supply. Plenty of bicarbonate too. There'll be many a dyspeptic reveler headed my way tomorrow. Adhesive plaster, yes. Bandages, yes. And this salve, mighty beneficial when applied to bruises and black eyes . . . "

In his office, Sheriff Bart Whitney was instructing his deputies and permitting them a preview of his finery. He had dressed for the occasion, on his standards anyway. Broad-brimmed, snow-white Stetson, a shirt of sky-blue with ruffled front, black string necktie, maroon frock-coat with gold-edged lapels teamed with ash-grey pants tucked into the inevitable knee-length boots and, of course, the famous Whitney buscadero buckled about the increasing Whitney midriff, the ivory butts of the long-barreled pistols impressively in evidence.

"My presence at the church and at the reception will be deterrent against ruffianly conduct by any invited guests," he droned, while the deputies fidgeted impatiently. "To my aides, however, falls the duty of ensuring there'll be no disturbance in Main Street or in any of the saloons in hearing distance of the Savoy. Deal harshly with rowdies, men. Act swiftly. Get 'em off the street fast, lock 'em up and keep lockin' 'em up. No matter if we end up with a crowded county jail. The hotheads can be released tomorrow morning, but not before. My good friends Mayor Lingard, Yancey Dodd, Ralph Joel and Billy Clayton are relying on us to keep the peace on this bright and shining wedding day, and, by thunder, that's what we're gonna do."

While the peace-keeping force of Lamont was being briefed, so were the minions of the venal Billy Clayton. He too was dressed for the occasion, as were Archer Hallam, Faro Treen, Rufe Gellard and Quint Mole.

"Dan and Phil will stay on the job here along with the other staff," Clayton reminded them, nodding to Reeby and the bullet-headed barkeep, Phil Druce. "Now, if all goes well, it doesn't seem likely any of us'll be followed back here after we leave the Savoy with the diamond. But, just in case, Dan and Phil know what to do. Any tin badge suddenly arriving has to be stalled, not necessarily with violence, you understand. No sense tipping our hand. Just make sure I'm given time to stash the loot."

"Arch or I can separate the Denver woman from the pendant," Treen said confidently. "Whichever of us is close enough when the right time comes. But *we'll* need time too, don't forget. Can't rush a job like this, Billy."

"I'll need to study the clasp," explained Hallam. "Better if this bauble is lifted quietly, Billy. We can't just tear the thing off her."

"Whatever way you handle it is okay by me," said Clayton. "But remember to give us a high sign when you're ready. Then we'll move closer and give you cover, distract Chadwick and the Dodds if need be."

"We're gonna grab us a fortune all in one piece," leered the bouncer. "And right under Big Bart's nose."

"Bart's our insurance," grinned Clayton. "As far as he's concerned, we're all above suspicion." Chuckling derisively he added, "I wouldn't have it any other way."

"So that's the routine?" prodded Mole.

"You all know what's expected of you," nodded Clayton. "We'll go along to the church now."

In their room at the Hartigan Hotel, about to don the coats of their well-tailored suits, the trouble-shooters paused to trade scrutinies.

"We look," complained Stretch, "like a couple undertakers lookin' for a customer."

"No, we don't," Larry reassured him. "Respectable enough is how we look, respectable enough to get by."

The shirts were white, the neckwear properly austere, the pants well-cut and their boots shining from liberal applications of dubbin. They donned the coats and worked their arms to assure themselves they could move with ease, which beat looking like a couple of starched-up tailor's dummies. Stretch's thoughtful eyes then wandered to the chair on which their coiled shellbelts and holstered .45's had been placed.

"Guess it ain't the right thing," he remarked. "I mean goin' gun-hung to a hitchin' and a fancy party afterwards with our hoglegs showin'. And it don't seem like Clayton's bunch'll make trouble for Milo tonight. We've been sidin' him careful. Ain't been none of them tinhorns come in spittin' distance of his wheelchair."

"Still and all, if we go *anyplace* gunless, we're gonna feel part naked," mused Larry.

"Ain't that the truth," agreed Stretch. "I don't have to pack both of mine, but — uh . . ."

"Just so long as we take a couple of friends along," drawled Larry. "We likely won't need 'em. It'll be just so we feel ready. Don't want to look nervous, do we?"

"As well as lookin' nervous, I'd *feel* nervous," said Stretch.

"Well," shrugged Larry. "We might's well."

"Might's well," nodded Stretch.

They moved to the chair, eased Colts from holsters, checked their loading and, lefthanded, felt for that part of their black pants most suitable for concealment of those trusty weapons. Larry slid the fingers of his left hand between shirt and pants and, righthanded, inserted his pistol with the butt and trigger section protruding. Stretch followed his example. They then donned their coats and reached for their hats.

"Milo borrowed a rig," offered Stretch.

"What kind?" asked Larry.

"Surrey," said Stretch. "I'll drive. Room enough in back for Abby, her old man and his wheelchair if we stay up front."

"Sounds okay," said Larry.

"So . . . " prodded Stretch.

"So let's go to a weddin'," shrugged Larry.

They quit the hotel, moved around to the alley and found the team hitched to the surrey and Milo, looking somewhat clean-cut this afternoon, black-suited and well-barbered, being wheeled through the back doorway of the Pioneer building by his daughter, who had never looked better.

As easily as if he were a small child, Larry transferred the newspaperman from the wheelchair to the rear seat of the surrey. He then offered his arm to the bright-eyed bridesmaid.

"Allow me, purty lady."

"Don't turn her head," Milo begged in mock alarm.

"If we were maybe fifteen years younger, Stretch and me would be tradin' punches to decide which of us courts her," declared Larry.

"Stop making bad jokes," chided Abby, as he handed her into the vehicle. "I don't want to faze the bride by showing up for the wedding with my eyes red from blubbering like a dumb schoolgirl."

Having swung up to the seat and gathered the reins, the taller Texan frowned over his shoulder at Milo.

"What's she talkin' about?"

"Just being sentimental," Milo calmly explained.

"The trouble is I'd have a hard time choosing between you," lamented Abby, arranging the skirts of her gown.

"You might've guessed," said Milo. "You tearaways have been her heroes since she was knee-high."

Larry swung up beside Stretch, who released the brake and flicked the team with his reins. As the surrey proceeded along the alley toward the first turn-off to the chapel, he gruffly offered advice.

"Never waste yourself on the likes of us, Abby honey. You deserve better."

"Slick young gent like Elroy, for instance," suggested Stretch.

"Mister Elroy Joel is already in love," Abby said caustically. "With Mister Elroy Joel."

"It was just an idea," shrugged Larry. "To me, he seemed a likely beau for a girl like you."

They arrived at the chapel close

behind the J Bar people and were in time to see the brothers Joel enter through the main doorway. Others of that sizeable crowd began filing in. The Texans promptly lifted Milo out of the surrey and into his wheelchair and joined the hunt for seats, while Abby took her position beside the other bridesmaid. The Joels, local and visitors, took the pew reserved for them and, fashionably late, the bridal party arrived some little time later.

The family Chadwick of Denver made an impressive entrance, moving down the centre aisle to trade polite smiles with the Joels and take their places. Not so impressive was George Middleton's entrance. Following Myra and the Chadwicks down the aisle, moving with great care, he nevertheless tripped over a highly polished boot to his left. Sheriff Whitney withdrew his foot, but too late. The Reverend Saul Padgett frowned disapprovingly; some members of the gathering failed to suppress their mirth at the sight of the embarrassed George slumping across the sheriff's lap. Mercifully, the awkward scene was soon forgotten. George was securely seated, and without further mishap, when the organist sounded a warning chord. The people rose. Yancey Dodd's big moment had come.

Firmly convinced every eye was on him, oblivious to the lush beauty of his only child in her silken wedding gown, the bow-legged, slickered-up old cattleman escorted her down the aisle with stately tread and his leathery face fixed in an expression of fearsome dignity; had anybody laughed, he would probably have ordered his bride-daughter to hold on just a minute while he put his fist to that fool's big mouth. Happily, nobody laughed.

The bride and her father made it to the front end of the aisle. Yancey then squeezed her arm, stepped clear of her train and retreated to the seating space beside his wife, managing that maneouver without colliding with a bridesmaid. As Max took his place beside his wife-to-be, Elroy positioned himself on his other side. The best man was ready to offer support; he even remembered to feel at the vest pocket containing the all-important gold band.

At a signal from the preacher, Doc Parrish's spinster sister raised her hands from the keyboard of the harmonium.

"Dearly, beloved, dear friends of Lamont and welcome visitors, we are gathered together to witness the wedding of two fine young people, also the welding of the bonds of lasting friendship between two highly respected families of this county . . . "

And so the ceremony was under way, and, already, Stretch was bedeviled by a lump in his throat and Larry, not so much the sentimentalist, wondering if the remainder of this day would be trouble-free. He noted the jewelry of the ladies from Denver and St Louis and was reflecting the Block D boss may not have exaggerated the possibility of a robbery attempt.

George wasn't paying much attention to the ceremony. He only had eyes for Miss Claudette Joel. And Clayton and his cronies only had eyes for Hildegard Chadwick's sparkling pendant.

8

The Eyes Of Texas

BY 4.30 p.m. the chapel was empty and the festive crowd filling the banquet room of the Savoy, a line of bachelors forming to kiss the happy bride, thirsty guests patronizing the well-stocked bar or crooking fingers at busy drink waiters. In a corner, Milo was settled comfortably in his wheelchair, nursing a drink and socializing with a trio of his old friends. Noting Clayton and his men were staying clear of the newspaperman, the Texans mutually agreed they could concentrate their attention on the awkward young man who had introduced himself to Claudette Joel; they weren't about to forget George's close call outside the *Pioneer* office.

At the insistence of the bride's

father, all obligatory speeches were delivered at this time, his idea being that the wedding banquet should be uninterrupted by 'all that palaverin'.'

Mayor Lingard led off by appointing himself master of ceremonies and delivering a speech of welcome which developed into a lengthy accolade directed at 'two of this county's leading families.' The recent feud was referred to and both ranchers praised for bringing it to a non-violent conclusion — with practical assistance from Mr and Mrs Max Joel.

Yancey was upright and vocal for some considerable time, though he began with an assurance he would speak only briefly. He, like many other inept orators, had plenty to say, but no idea of how to summarize, how to bring a speech to an end, and so he was on his feet a full 10 minutes.

Not so long-winded were Ralph Joel, the bride and the best man. Friends and relatives were warmly thanked for their wedding gifts and, with great elan,

Elroy paid the customary compliments to the bridesmaids.

Speeches and champagne having set an edge to their appetites, the guests were only too ready to begin partaking of the banquet prepared by the Savoy's chef and staff; the eating began around 6 p.m., by which time the Branding Iron, located directly opposite the hotel, had filled with Block D and J Bar hands. Thus, while the invited wedding guests celebrated sedately in the Savoy's grand dining room, other well-wishers were holding a somewhat noisier celebration just across the street.

Though they satisfied their appetites and downed their share of the fine liquor provided, Larry and Stretch kept their eyes busy. Backing his hunch as to why young George had been marked for elimination, Larry kept a wary eye on that smitten bachelor now seated beside laughing-eyed Claudette. For Stretch's eyes, there could be only one target; like many others here present, he was fascinated by the shining bauble displayed on the well-curved frontage of the lady from Denver.

When that exotic banquet finally ended, the Savoy's four-piece orchestra appeared to the accompaniment of a round of applause and proceeded to the dais at the street-end of the room. The music began. The bridal couple waltzed for the admiration of the crowd, after which other couples took the floor, Yancey partnering Amy Joel, her husband partnering Myra Dodd, Elroy requesting the pleasure of dancing with Abby, Jerome Chadwick descending on Stella Joel and his wife graciously consenting to partner Lester. This was George's cue. He had been dreading this moment, but was captivated by Claudette; to favorably impress her, he would make any sacrifice.

"May I have the honor, Miss Joel?"

"Claudette," she insisted, rising and taking his arm. "Let's not be formal, George. I find your company most agreeable."

"You're too kind, Claudette," he mumbled, steeling himself for the ordeal. "And I hope you'll continue to be kind. I am, you see, somewhat of a tanglefoot, an inept dancer at best."

"All you need is confidence," she smiled.

"If I could be as confident as you," he said wistfully, "as poised, as assured . . . "

"I wasn't always this way," she confided.

"I find that hard to believe," he protested.

"It's the truth, George," she declared. "I'd be the wallflower of this wonderful party, sitting in a corner by myself and praying nobody would notice me, if I weren't wearing my Wolf Tooth charm. He was a warrior chief, you see, and I'm under his influence."

George searched his mind for suitable rejoinder. The best he could manage was,

"That's — quite interesting."

Gingerly, he squired her onto the dance floor.

"Remember Wolf Tooth," she urged. "And relax. We'll just move in time with the music and enjoy ourselves."

If he had doubts about Wolf Tooth's influence, he had none about Claudette's. With her in his arms, he waltzed with all the aplomb, all the grace of a Hussar. They joined the other dancers gracefully circling the ballroom, and Cordeau was watching and waiting, sensing his moment was at hand.

Twilight having passed, the ballroom was now ablaze with light. Mayor Lingard's pride and joy, the ornate chandelier freighted in from Chicago a year ago, hovered above the twirling couples in glittery majesty. Cordeau deftly delivered wine to a seated couple, but without taking his eyes off his intended victim. Waltzing with the mayor's rotund wife, Sheriff Whitney beetled his brows to the alien sound of gunshots and muttered a reassurance.

"Don't worry, ma'am. That'll be unruly cowboys letting off steam. My deputies have their orders. The offenders will be disarmed and taken to jail in a matter of moments."

A half-dozen or more ranch-hands, four Block D men and a couple of J Bar waddies, had stumbled out of the Branding Iron much the worse for booze and were raising a racket, discharging their pistols to the evening sky, ignoring the bellowed reprimand of Deputy Mat Rockwell, who was a full half-block away at this moment. In the ballroom, the gun-thunder intruded through the open windows, the din drowning the music, causing some of the out-of-towners to grimace in annoyance. It persisted to the point that Whitney felt compelled to make a token gesture. He politely requested Blanche Lingard to step clear of him, turned and drew his famous pistols. Stella Joel promptly screamed and three other women made it a strident quartet.

"There is no need for alarm, ladies!"

boomed Whitney. "I'll deal with those trigger-happy roughnecks!"

The sheriff's grandstand play and the continuing uproar of gunfire were all the incentive Cordeau needed. He had gotten rid of his empty tray, drawn his .38 and had it concealed by a bar-cloth when the tall Texan lounging by a window became interested. From George, Larry's gaze switched to the drink-waiter. He noted George's back was turned and that the waiter was darting wary glances to right and left, as he moved clear of the window and began his advance. He had to dodge to avoid colliding with the dancers, but his eyes were on Cordeau's right forearm when the unexpected happened and his suspicion was confirmed.

It was a freak accident, the kind of reversal Cordeau could never have anticipated. Just as he drew a bead on his target, a waltzing couple came twirling past. Stella Joel was laughing gaily, Jerome Chadwick energetically whirling her, so much so that the full skirts of her gown, boosted by several petticoats, swished up and struck one end of the folded towel draped over Cordeau's gunhand, whisking it away. For an anguished moment, Cordeau froze. Larry got one hand behind him, threw up his coattails and, while whipping out his Colt, yelled at Cordeau to drop his weapon. Cordeau reacted rashly, swinging the weapon toward him.

With no dancers separating him from his adversary, Larry crouched and fired. His well-aimed bullet shallowly creased the killer's left shoulder and started him lurching backward. Cordeau was falling when his trigger-finger contracted. The Smith & Wesson barked and the slug went high, tearing a hole in the ballroom ceiling.

The effect of these close-at-hand shots was chaotic. People scattered in disorder, some of them losing their footing.

"By Dawg!" whooped Yancey. "I

knew I could count on them Texas bucks!"

Regaining his balance, Cordeau sighted his partner and yelled to him.

"Cover me, damn it! We got to get out of here!"

Barris promptly tossed his tray aside, drew his pistol and triggered two shots over the heads of the scattering people, roaring,

"Don't anybody get in our way!"

Abby suddenly found herself prone with Elroy sprawled half across her.

"Stay down!" he gasped in her ear. "If one of us has to stop a wild bullet, better me than you!"

"This is — very heroic," she panted. "You're shielding me at — at risk to yourself."

"Do the same for any woman I loved," he muttered. "Besides, I probably heal faster than you."

"Don't be flippant and heroic at the same time," she chided. "And don't pretend you aren't frightened."

"I'm frightened," he said bluntly,

"but only for you."

Elroy's decisive action was repeated by George, if more clumsily. Claudette hit the floor in a flurry of skirts and lace petticoats after George's knee struck the back of her calves. Then, to her confusion, he was on his knees and flopping over her.

"George — *really* — !"

"Please don't m-m-misunderstand!" he pleaded. "I couldn't bear for you to be — struck down by gunfire — my dear Claudette!"

"This is so sudden," she remarked.

"So is a bullet," he winced.

Clayton and his men were quick to take advantage of the uproar, moving according to plan, but with at least one guest keeping them in view. A panic-stricken guest had separated Lester Joel from the fair Hildegard, colliding with him so forcibly that he was sent sprawling. Quint Mole promptly took the Denver lady's arm, distracting her while Archer Hallam moved up behind her and deftly unfastened the chain from which her pendant hung.

"Allow me, ma'am," Mole said smoothly. "We'd best get you clear of this disturbance."

"My husband . . . " she began.

"We'll find him for you," offered Clayton, watching Hallam retreat to an archway with Treen and Gellard following.

Hildegard was ushered to a chair. And only then, when she was about to seat herself, did she note her loss. Her anguished cry caused Clayton and his minions to make themselves scarce, unaware the taller Texan was struggling his way toward them. People kept getting in Stretch's way, but he wasn't losing sight of the exit through which Clayton and Company had disappeared.

The killers too were in flight. Barris had temporarily stalled Larry, sliding a chair his way, causing him to trip and sprawl. When he made it to his feet and began pursuing them, the sheriff was dominating the centre of the ballroom, still brandishing his gleaming pistols and assuring the gathering his deputies had the situation in hand — while scaring hell out of the female guests.

"Just keep dancin', folks!" urged Stretch. "Just keep dancin'!"

The chef and his helpers were thrown into panic when, after their hectic descent, Cordeau and Barris charged through the hotel kitchen to the rear door. No sooner had they made their exit than Larry appeared, hefting his Colt and growling at everybody to stay right where they were.

Emerging into the back alley, sighting the fleeing duo, he called his challenge.

"That's far enough! Drop your guns!"

Their reaction was exactly as he expected. Two to one. Their idea of sure-fire odds. Unhampered by his grazed shoulder, his gunarm as lethal as ever, Cordeau turned as Barris turned. Both cut loose, but no faster than Larry. He felt the tugging sensation and caught the smell of bullet-seared cloth at his left side as he returned Cordeau's shot and put him down. Barris' bullet fanned his right ear as he crouched and fired again, and then Barris was spinning with his gunarm bloody, dropping his weapon. Off-balance, he came up hard against a wall, striking it face-first, then flopping unconscious.

Hurried footsteps caused Larry to whirl, ready to protect himself again. Jud Berry, Whitney's other deputy, was an arm's length and about to mouth a challenge when Larry got his left hand to his holster and deftly emptied it.

"Hired killers is my guess, Deputy," he said briskly. "Stash 'em different cells, savvy? Keep 'em well separated and, if one of 'em's cashed in, don't let the other know it. Tell the live one his partner confessed everything . . ."

"That way, maybe you'll learn who was payin' 'em to kill George Middleton," offered Larry, starting for the south corner.

"My iron . . . !" the deputy called after him.

"Don't worry," said Larry. "It's just a loan."

When he reached Main Street, eight disarmed and inebriated cowboys were en route to the county jail, prodded along by Deputy Rockwell and a barkeep from the Branding Iron, both hefting shotguns. Stretch was in plain sight a half-block away, beckoning him. He began running and, moments later, was joining his partner in the mouth of the alley this side of the Clayton Casino.

"They snuck in the back way," Stretch reported.

"What the hell . . . ?" began Larry.

Stretch cut the question short.

"Clayton, the bouncer and three other bastards we tangled with. One of 'em grabbed the Denver lady's diamond — and I'm the only one knows. They worked so slick . . . "

"There were two killers tryin' for the boy from Kansas," muttered Larry. "A deputy's got 'em now — so I'm kind of available again. You ready to separate Clayton's bunch from the jewelry?" He added a prediction. "They'll likely make a fight of it."

"That's never discouraged us before, not that I recall," growled Stretch. "Whichaway, runt?"

"This is a day for back doors," decided Larry.

"Whatever you say," shrugged Stretch.

They ran to the rear end of the alley, turned left and advanced on the back door. It was locked, but locked doors were no more deterrent than heavy odds. This one surrendered to the impact of their combined weight, and then they were barging through a storeroom and into the casino.

The fact that they both brandished guns caused the few patrons present to make a rush for the batwings. The percentage-girls, equally intimidated, followed the neutrals out. That left the bartenders, one of whom, Druce, had dropped his hands below the bar, and the suddenly impassive Dan Reeby, seated alone at a table near the stairs.

"All upstairs, huh?" Larry challenged the barkeeps.

"Who?" growled Druce.

"Your boss and the rest of 'em," said Stretch, his eyes on Reeby. "Them that lifted the Denver lady's trinket."

"That's a stupid accusation," drawled Reeby. "And you can forget about upstairs. It's out of bounds to proddy saddlebums."

"You hear what the sharper said?" Stretch asked Larry.

"Nary a word," said Larry. "Guess I'm deaf from all that shootin' at the hotel."

As they started for the stairs, Druce brought a shotgun into view and worked both hammers back; Reeby's right hand suddenly filled with a Remington derringer, its muzzles lined on Stretch, who promptly sidestepped with his colt booming. Simultaneously, Larry cut loose at Druce; his bullet creased the barkeep's skull, driving him back against the glassware-laden shelves with the scattergun blasting upward, the double charge doing ugly things to the Palace's ornately decorated ceiling. Reeby, his right shoulder broken by Stretch's slug, back-somersaulted out of his chair and sprawled, his sneak-pistol skittering away from him, face contorted.

Ignoring the other bartenders, the Texans took to the stairs. They reached the gallery just as a door opened and Faro Treen stepped out, his right hand gunfilled. Stretch gave him no time to cock the weapon, much less use it. His Colt roared again. The impact of the slug that wrecked his right arm turned Treen and drove him against the rail, against and over it. He yelled as he pitched into the area below, but stopped yelling after crashing onto the table that collapsed under him.

First to dive through the doorway, Larry caught a blurred impression of Clayton's handsomely appointed office, Clayton on one knee beside the open safe, Hallam at the open window with gun leveled, Gellard and Mole filled their hands. Hallam fired and missed and became Larry's first target; he triggered fast and with deadly accuracy and, with the .45 slug in his heart, Hallam hurtled backward through the window to collapse on the balcony. Armed now, aiming a pistol at Larry, Clayton didn't get to squeeze trigger. Stretch's bullet struck him dead centre. Buffeted by a slug gouging at his left thigh, Larry lurched with his gun booming. Mole loosed a wail and went down just as the bouncer discharged his pistol at Stretch, but not as fast as Stretch flopped with his Colt roaring again. When he hit the floor, Gellard was as dead as Clayton and Hallam.

Larry's face, contorted by pain, was a fearsome sight for the groaning Mole to behold. He shuddered to the feel of a Colt's muzzle prodding his chin.

"I'll ask it once!" breathed Larry. "Where'd Clayton stash the diamond?"

"He — didn't get to — stash it!"

gasped Mile. "He only now unlocked the safe!"

"Check," ordered Larry.

Stretch rolled Clayton's body over, explored an inside pocket and grim-faced, retrieved the bauble.

"Why do females got to wear these damn treasures?" he grouched. "This is the kind of wealth fools die for."

"We're goin' back to the Savoy," muttered Larry, limping to the window.

"You're leakin' blood," warned Stretch, as if he hadn't noticed.

"I won't leak it on Mayor Lingard's fancy ballroom," shrugged Larry. "It better be you gives the lady what these heroes took from her."

They were gone from the back alley by the time Deputy Rockwell and a handful of townmen entered the Casino from Main Street to investigate the shooting. Only by luck did they reach the Savoy undetected by the other deputy. As they climbed the stairs to the ballroom, Larry moving with difficulty, knotting a bandana about his thigh, they heard the strains of a Strauss waltz and traded wry grins.

"That's real nice," remarked Stretch. "The folks gettin' back to their dancin' and celebratin'. Too bad, there had to be a ruckus here, but I guess nobody's worryin' no more."

From the entrance to the banquet hall, propped up by his left shoulder, Larry watched his self-conscious partner move past the waltzing couples, steering a course for Hildegard Chadwick, who was accepting three fingers of brandy from the solicitous Ralph Joel. He let his gaze stray just long enough to observe a quite graceful George partnering Claudette again, she smiling into his face and the just as happy Abby dancing unconventionally close to Elroy, chuckling as he kissed her ear.

According beautiful Hildegard a jerky bow, Stretch proffered the recovered pendant. The Dodds and the St Louis Joels drew closer as he mumbled an apology.

"Here's your purty jewelry, ma'am.

I'm mighty sorry it took so long gettin' back to you, but some hombres that stole it — uh — gave us quite an argument."

"Hey, how about this!" grinned Yancey. "By Dawg, you could bet the Texas Helions'd settle their hash"

"I am," Hildegard said softly, "most grateful."

"You and your friend — at great risk to your lives . . . " began her husband.

"Just did what needed doin'," shrugged Stretch.

"Our esteemed sheriff obviously has the wrong idea," frowned Ralph Joel.

"About what?" demanded the mayor. He was rejoining the group after supervising the removal of broken glass and damaged chairs and had not yet recovered from the shock of seeing the reception briefly deteriorate to a shambles. "Just what is Whitney *doing* about this outrage — that's what *I* want to know! It's not enough for him to wave those pistols about and make heroic speeches! What of the men responsible for that fracas?"

He winced and sidestepped. In his haste to gather details for a special edition, Milo Fenner had wheeled himself to the group and buffeted the mayor's shins.

"Sorry about that, Gene. You were saying, Mister Joel?"

"Apparently there was gunplay in the back alley, Mister Fenner," said Joel. "I get the impression that this tall gentleman and his friend are well known to Bart and . . . "

"And Bart's decided they're responsible for the whole hullabaloo," guessed Milo.

"He demanded they be arrested on sight," said Joel. "Yancey, Jerry, that doesn't seem quite fair, you agree? So, shall we accompany the wrongly-accused to the sheriff's office and get this little matter straightened out?"

"The least we can do," insisted Jerome. "Hildegard, my dear, if you'll excuse us . . . ?"

"Stretch, wheel me," begged Milo. "I have to be in *this*."

As the mayor, the two cattlemen and Jerome Chadwick approached, followed by Stretch pushing Milo's wheelchair, Larry's vision began blurring. He mumbled a curse, feeling disgruntled now, irritated by his sudden weakness. In the moment before he passed out, he acknowledged the logic of it. You get creased, lose blood, you just naturally pass out. Was he not human after all?

When he regained consciousness, he was sprawled on the couch in the law office. Stretch was hunkered beside him, securing his pants belt.

"Howdy, runt," he grunted. "I had to half strip you so that Doc could patch your wound."

"Any females here?" mumbled Larry.

"Nope," grinned Stretch. "There, you're decent again now. Stay quiet and I'll fetch you a shot of Big Butt's booze."

Propping himself on an elbow, gazing about him, Larry saw Doc Parrish close by, returning instruments to his valise and looking as mournful as ever. Deputy Berry lounged in the entrance to the ground floor cellblock. Obviously he had retrieved his six-gun; it was back in his holster. Filling the chair behind his desk, Sheriff Bart Whitney was striving to mask his perplexity, but not succeeding. He seemed more confused than outraged when Stretch crouched beside him to explore his desk-drawers. Milo, taking the air in the street-doorway, puffing on a cigar, chuckled approvingly as Stretch found what he sought, removed its cork and half-filled a glass. The glass was taken to his partner, who put a couple of generous mouthfuls right where they would to the most good.

"Billy Clayton . . . " Whitney voiced the name with much head shaking and mustache-stroking. "A man I trusted, a man I thought worthy of my friendship, now revealed as a scheming rogue. Gentlemen, I am deeply affected by this — uh — this great shock."

"Life is full of surprises," Milo said unsympathetically. To Larry, he drawled an assurance. "Don't worry. You and Stretch have come out of this fracas with your reputation unsullied."

"I wasn't worryin'" shrugged Larry.

"Stay off that leg," advised Parrish, sagging into a spare chair. "A couple of days at least. Too early for you to think of leaving town anyway. You'll be required to swear statements for the sheriff's information — and that'll probably take time."

"Messers Dodd, Joel, Chadwick and the mayor have returned to the reception," offered Milo. "They're probably dancing again now. Of course they spoke on your behalf and the sheriff now realizes you weren't the instigators of this disruption. However, he still has questions. I can tell — from the look on his noble visage."

"So go ahead and ask, Sheriff," urged Larry. "My partner and me got nothin' to hide."

"Deputy Berry . . . " sighed Whitney.

"Yessir, glad to oblige," nodded the deputy.

"If I may make a suggestion," said Milo.

"Mister Fenner?" frowned Berry.

"It might clear the air if you first tell our Texas friends of your telegraph message to the Shadlow sheriff," said Milo. "And, of course, your reason for doing so."

"That should come first, you think?" prodded Berry.

"The law should be scrupulously fair with Larry and Stretch," Milo opined in mock solemnity. "The law owes them so much, when all is said and done."

"Whatever you say, Mister Fenner," nodded the deputy. To Larry, he explained, "Those two strangers you fought behind the hotel were a couple professional killers. I identified 'em from our files. Name of Emile Cordeau and Carl Barris. I had 'em toted here and — you gave me an idea, remember?"

"It worked," guessed Larry.

"Barris was the live one," said Berry. "I stashed him upstairs, left the dead one to the undertaker. Then, after the other doc brought Barris around, I claimed I got a statement from Cordeau."

"Jud played it sneaky, it seems," grinned Milo. "Told Barris his partner claimed he never did any killing. Cordeau is supposed to have called Barris the brains of the partnership."

"That hit Barris hard," said Berry.

"That's why I wired the Shadlow sheriff," said Berry. "Barris named the woman who hired 'em to get rid of the young cashier feller. She's the widow of a rancher name of McQueen. His foreman, Keesing, is the chief suspect. McQueen was stabbed to death and the cashier saw Keesing running away."

"Rockwell also secured a signed confession," offered Milo. "When the chips are down, there's always a coward who'll crack. Faro Treen admitted he was one of my assailants. The others were Gellard, Mole and Hallam — and Clayton put 'em up to it. Of course it was Clayton devised the plan to snatch the Kuruman diamond."

"Billy Clayton," Whitney said dolefully. "A murderous rogue — masquerading as my friend. This is a sad night for me."

"Now *I* got a question," said Berry, staring hard at Larry. "Emerson's told us he spotted Clayton's men snatch the diamond. That's why you hot shots called that showdown at the casino. No question about that. But this Middleton thing is something else. How could you *know*, Valentine? You were watching Cordeau at the party. You were onto him already."

"Wrong," said Larry. "I was watchin' young George, so naturally I was ready when the killer showed his hogleg."

"But how'd you know Middleton was in danger?" demanded Berry.

"It was just a hunch," Larry said mildly. "I rode out to Block D one night, the night Doc gave George a lift, and we got to talking. Young feller said as how he'd be the only witness against Keesing."

"And that made you leery?" challenged Berry. "Damn it, that's far-fetched."

"You got to remember we've been messin' with killers a long time — all kinds of killers," drawled Stretch.

"This ain't the first killer with a friend," Larry assured the deputy. "Kind of friend who'd spend mucho dinero to save him from a hangrope? We've known of others like George."

"The famous Valentine sixth sense," remarked Milo. "Jud, if I were you, I'd leave it at that." Berry looked at his chief. Whitney heaved a sigh and gestured in dismissal. "Fine. So, if somebody'll wheel me to my office, I have quite an edition to prepare. I think I'll leave it to Abby to write up the wedding. I'll be happily busy setting up my story of the foiled attempt on young Middleton's life, the theft and recovery of a famous gem and the decisive defeat of the guilty parties."

Neither Texan felt inclined to rejoin the celebration at the Savoy. With help from Doc Parrish, Larry made it to the double at the Hartigan. The medico relieved him of his boots, after which he flopped on the nearest bed and fell asleep.

The celebration was transferred to the railroad depot at 11.45 p.m. and the bridal couple accorded a rousing send-off. Dodds, Joels and guests then wended their way homeward and their sore-headed employees were released from the county jail to find their horses and do likewise. The groom's father was still voicing his regrets that the festivities had been marred by violence and bloodshed. Not so the bride's father, whose wish had been granted; this had been one of Yancey Dodd's best days.

It was late when the St Louis Joels prepared for sleep in the fine bedroom assigned to them in the stately J Bar ranch-house, but Stella was still in good voice.

"My nerves are shattered, my ears still throbbing from that dreadful din," she complained. "The gunfire, the screams, the disgraceful commotion . . . "

"Ralph and Amy have apologized," Lester reminded her. "Not that they're in any way responsible."

"I suppose, on frontier standards, the whole hectic affair should be regarded as a great success," sniffed Stella.

"Old Yancey Dodd seemed remarkably happy," frowned Lester.

They donned robes when their daughter knocked and called to them. She was invited to enter, and did so with her face wreathed in smiles, her eyes aglow. Claudette had a request. Could they prolong their Lamont visit, at least until it came time for George to return to Shadlow, Kansas? This request prompted the predictable question. Who was George? Excitedly, Claudette recounted the young cashier's spectacular act of gallantry.

"He knocked my legs from under me and sprawled over me!"

"He — *what* . . . ?" wailed Stella, clasping hand to breast.

"During the shooting — at the party? To protect me, he pushed me to the floor and actually shielded me with his own body. Isn't that the bravest, noblest thing you ever heard of?"

"What kind of man . . . ?" began Stella.

"I think I remember him," soothed Lester. "I doubt if he'd behave that way under normal circumstances . . . "

"I should hope!" gasped Stella.

"Seemed a diffident young fellow," recalled Lester. "Quite harmless, really."

"He's junior cashier of a bank in Shadlow and he intends asking your permission to court me," bragged Claudette. "And that'll be just wonderful. I'm going to enjoy being courted by George. I'm so happy about George that I don't really mind losing it."

"Losing . . . ?" breathed Stella.

"My Wolf Tooth medallion," said Claudette. "It must've broken free of the strap during all the hullabaloo. We searched, George and I, but couldn't find it anywhere."

"Now, Claudette," said Lester, studying her intently. "This surely doesn't mean you'll — uh — lose all the confidence, the high spirits, the good humor you've expressed since we acquired that cheap bauble — does it?"

Turning to leave the room, Claudette said very calmly,

"I don't think I could be shy again. Being confident is more fun. And George so admires my confidence. He's a trifle clumsy and, though we're only getting to know each other, I feel he relies on me. Yes, I feel George needs me and, of course, I can't disappoint him."

With that, she retired to her own room, leaving her parents to hope for the best.

The Chadwicks of Denver, in the privacy of their bedroom at Block D, talked briefly before retiring. Their expressions were pensive as they gazed at the recovered pendant now being returned to Hildegard's jewel box.

"Are we responsible, do you think?" frowned the blonde beauty. "Jerry, darling, men have been shot. There were fatalities, and all because . . . "

"You're over-simplifying," Jerome gently chided. "We are in no way responsible, I assure you. Did we call in the Denver press and announce to the whole country you'd be wearing the Kuruman at this wedding? Obviously the thieves assumed you'd do so and, having reached that assumption, there was no holding them back. Just one thing though, my dear. I don't feel any obligation to let it be known we brought the paste replica to Lamont and left the genuine diamond in the strongroom at the Denver Trust Bank."

"What people don't know can't hurt them?" she smiled.

"Exactly," he nodded. "And, here in Lamont, who'd detect the difference? On you, it looked magnificent."

Because Larry chose to remain in

Lamont until his wound was completely healed the Texas Drifters took their leave several days after the departure of the Denver and St Louis visitors. As was their usual routine, they purchased necessary supplies, saddled their animals and left town quietly. The only local accorded a personal adios was the founder-editor of the *Pioneer*, who was somewhat intrigued by their parting gift.

"Lethal looking thing," he remarked, gingerly inspecting the weapon. "Mighty thoughtful of you just the same, boys. I presume I should use it as a paper-knife or a cigar cutter. How'd you come by it — do you mind my asking? I've seen none like it in any local store."

"You ain't suppose to ask," said Stretch. "All you need to know is . . . "

"The hombre that owned it won't be usin' it any more," drawled Larry. "That's all, scribbler. Take care now. Hope you'll be out of that chair and on your own two feet plenty soon."

"Where do we find Abby?" asked Stretch.

"You've missed her," said Milo, winking slyly. "My daughter and her beau packed a picnic basket, borrowed a J Bar buggy and took a ride to who knows where."

"So it's gonna be Abby and Elroy?" prodded Larry.

"Looks that way," nodded Milo. "So all's well that ends well. The young tanglefoot from Kansas is back in his hometown by now. I'll wire the Shadlow law for the verdict in the Keesing trial, though there can be no doubt he'll be convicted. Meant to tell you. Thought you'd be interested. The murder victim's widow . . . "

"Her that paid Cordeau and his partner to butcher George?" scowled Larry.

"Whitney got word from the Shadlow sheriff late yesterday," offered Milo. "She too will be held for trial. Conspiracy in the murder of her husband. Conspiracy in the attempted murder of the prosecution witness. The Barris jasper spilled it all. Apparently Cordeau made more than one attempt to kill the witness."

"Like Larry always says," remarked Stretch. "Everybody gets what's comin' to 'em."

"Where to from here?" asked Milo, as the tall men nodded so-long and made for the doorway.

"Someplace where we can take it easy and stay out of trouble," said Larry.

"There's no such place," frowned Milo.

Larry moved out to the waiting horses. The taller Texan paused on the threshold just long enough to glance back at the newspaperman and draw a rejoinder.

"Ain't that the truth."

Books by Marshall Grover
in the Linford Western Library:

BANDIT BAIT
EMERSON'S HIDEOUT
HEROES AND HELLERS
GHOST-WOMAN OF CASTILLO
THE DEVIL'S DOZEN
HELL IN HIGH COUNTRY
TEN FAST HORSES
SAVE A BULLET FOR KEEHOE
DANGER RODE DRAG
THE KILLERS WORE BLACK
REUNION IN SAN JOSE
CORMACK CAME BACK
RESCUE PARTY
KINCAID'S LAST RIDE
7 FOR BANNER PASS
THE HELLION BREED
THE TRUTH ABOUT SNAKE RIDGE
DEVIL'S DINERO
HARTIGAN
SHOTGUN SHARKEY
THE LOGANTOWN LOOTERS
THE SEVENTH GUILTY MAN
BULLET FOR A WIDOW

CALABOOSE EXPRESS
WHISKEY GULCH
THE ALIBI TRAIL
SIX GUILTY MEN
FORT DILLON
IN PURSUIT OF QUINCEY BUDD
HAMMER'S HORDE
TWO GENTLEMEN FROM TEXAS
HARRIGAN'S STAR
TURN THE KEY ON EMERSON
ROUGH ROUTE TO RODD COUNTY
SEVEN KILLERS EAST
DAKOTA DEATH-TRAP
GOLD, GUNS AND THE GIRL
RUCKUS AT GILA WELLS
LEGEND OF COYOTE FORD
ONE HELL OF A SHOWDOWN
EMERSON'S HEX

Other titles in the Linford Western Library:

TOP HAND
Wade Everett

The Broken T was big. But no ranch is big enough to let a man hide from himself.

GUN WOLVES OF LOBO BASIN
Lee Floren

The Feud was a blood debt. When Smoke Talbot found the outlaws who gunned down his folks he aimed to nail their hide to the barn door.

SHOTGUN SHARKEY
Marshall Grover

The westbound coach carrying the indomitable Larry and Stretch headed for a shooting showdown.

FIGHTING RAMROD
Charles N. Heckelmann

Most men would have cut their losses, but Frazer counted the bullets in his guns and said he'd soak the range in blood before he'd give up another inch of what was his.

LONE GUN
Eric Allen

Smoke Blackbird had been away too long. The Lequires had seized the Blackbird farm, forcing the Indians and settlers off, and no one seemed willing to fight! He had to fight alone.

THE THIRD RIDER
Barry Cord

Mel Rawlins wasn't going to let anything stand in his way. His father was murdered, his two brothers gone. Now Mel rode for vengeance.

ARIZONA DRIFTERS
W. C. Tuttle

When drifting Dutton and Lonnie Steelman decide to become partners they find that they have a common enemy in the formidable Thurston brothers.

TOMBSTONE
Matt Braun

Wells Fargo paid Luke Starbuck to outgun the silver-thieving stagecoach gang at Tombstone. Before long Luke can see the only thing bearing fruit in this eldorado will be the gallows tree.

HIGH BORDER RIDERS
Lee Floren

Buckshot McKee and Tortilla Joe cut the trail of a border tough who was running Mexican beef into Texas. They stopped the smuggler in his tracks.

BRETT RANDALL, GAMBLER
E. B. Mann

Larry Day had the choice of running away from the law or of assuming a dead man's place. No matter what he decided he was bound to end up dead.

THE GUNSHARP
William R. Cox

The Eggerleys weren't very smart. They trained their sights on Will Carney and Arizona's biggest blood bath began.

THE DEPUTY OF SAN RIANO
Lawrence A. Keating and Al. P. Nelson

When a man fell dead from his horse, Ed Grant was spotted riding away from the scene. The deputy sheriff rode out after him and came up against everything from gunfire to dynamite.

FARGO: MASSACRE RIVER
John Benteen

The ambushers up ahead had now blocked the road. Fargo's convoy was a jumble, a perfect target for the insurgents' weapons!

SUNDANCE: DEATH IN THE LAVA
John Benteen

The Modoc's captured the wagon train and its cargo of gold. But now the halfbreed they called Sundance was going after it . . .

HARSH RECKONING
Phil Ketchum

Five years of keeping himself alive in a brutal prison had made Brand tough and careless about who he gunned down . . .

FARGO: PANAMA GOLD
John Benteen

With foreign money behind him, Buckner was going to destroy the Panama Canal before it could be completed. Fargo's job was to stop Buckner.

FARGO: THE SHARPSHOOTERS
John Benteen

The Canfield clan, thirty strong were raising hell in Texas. Fargo was tough enough to hold his own against the whole clan.

PISTOL LAW
Paul Evan Lehman

Lance Jones came back to Mustang for just one thing — revenge! Revenge on the people who had him thrown in jail.

HELL RIDERS
Steve Mensing

Wade Walker's kid brother, Duane, was locked up in the Silver City jail facing a rope at dawn. Wade was a ruthless outlaw, but he was smart, and he had vowed to have his brother out of jail before morning!

DESERT OF THE DAMNED
Nelson Nye

The law was after him for the murder of a marshal — a murder he didn't commit. Breen was after him for revenge — and Breen wouldn't stop at anything . . . blackmail, a frameup . . . or murder.

DAY OF THE COMANCHEROS
Steven C. Lawrence

Their very name struck terror into men's hearts — the Comancheros, a savage army of cutthroats who swept across Texas, leaving behind a bloodstained trail of robbery and murder.

SUNDANCE: SILENT ENEMY
John Benteen

A lone crazed Cheyenne was on a personal war path. They needed to pit one man against one crazed Indian. That man was Sundance.

LASSITER
Jack Slade

Lassiter wasn't the kind of man to listen to reason. Cross him once and he'll hold a grudge for years to come — if he let you live that long.

LAST STAGE TO GOMORRAH
Barry Cord

Jeff Carter, tough ex-riverboat gambler, now had himself a horse ranch that kept him free from gunfights and card games. Until Sturvesant of Wells Fargo showed up.

McALLISTER ON THE COMANCHE CROSSING

Matt Chisholm

The Comanche, McAllister owes them a life — and the trail is soaked with the blood of the men who had tried to outrun them before.

QUICK-TRIGGER COUNTRY

Clem Colt

Turkey Red hooked up with Curly Bill Graham's outlaw crew. But wholesale murder was out of Turk's line, so when range war flared he bucked the whole border gang alone . . .

CAMPAIGNING

Jim Miller

Ambushed on the Santa Fe trail, Sean Callahan is saved by two Indian strangers. But there'll be more lead and arrows flying before the band join Kit Carson against the Comanches.

GUNSLINGER'S RANGE
Jackson Cole

Three escaped convicts are out for revenge. They won't rest until they put a bullet through the head of the dirty snake who locked them behind bars.

RUSTLER'S TRAIL
Lee Floren

Jim Carlin knew he would have to stand up and fight because he had staked his claim right in the middle of Big Ike Outland's best grass.

THE TRUTH ABOUT SNAKE RIDGE
Marshall Grover

The troubleshooters came to San Cristobal to help the needy. For Larry and Stretch the turmoil began with a brawl and then an ambush.

WOLF DOG RANGE
Lee Floren

at nothing,
d him first
te Manly's

DEVIL'S DINERO
Marshall Grover

Plagued by remorse, a rich old reprobate hired the Texas Trouble-shooters to deliver a fortune in greenbacks to each of his victims.

GUNS OF FURY
Ernest Haycox

Dane Starr, alias Dan Smith, wanted to close the door on his past and hang up his guns, but people wouldn't let him.